Jimfish

Also by Christopher Hope

NOVELS

A Separate Development
Kruger's Alp
The Hottentot Room
My Chocolate Redeemer
Serenity House
Me, the Moon and Elvis Presley
Darkest England
Heaven Forbid
My Mother's Lovers
Shooting Angels

SHORT STORIES

The Love Songs of Nathan J. Swirsky
Learning to Fly
The Garden of Bad Dreams

NON-FICTION

White Boy Running
Moscow, Moscow
Signs of the Heart
Brothers under the Skin: Travels in Tyranny

POETRY

Cape Drives
Englishmen
In the Country of the Black Pig

FOR CHILDREN

The King, the Cat and the Fiddle (with Yehudi Menuhin)
The Dragon Wore Pink

Christopher Hope

Jimfish

OR
TEN YEARS
ON THE WRONG
SIDE OF HISTORY

ATLANTIC BOOKS
LONDON

First published in Great Britain in 2015 by Atlantic Books,
an imprint of Atlantic Books Ltd.

This paperback edition published in Great Britain
in 2016 by Atlantic Books.

1 3 5 7 9 10 8 6 4 2

A CIP catalogue record for this book is available
from the British Library.

Paperback ISBN: 978 0 85789 807 4
E-book ISBN: 978 0 85789 808 1

Printed in Great Britain by Clays Ltd, St Ives plc

Atlantic Books
An imprint of Atlantic Books Ltd
Ormond House
26–27 Boswell Street
London WC1N 3JZ

www.atlantic-books.co.uk

To Bella, Blake, Antony

Like much else in *Jimfish*, not only are many
events all-too real – the collapse of ex-Yugoslavia,
the fall of the Berlin Wall, the red berets of the
Fifth Commando in Zimbabwe with their zeal for
massacres, Mobutu's many palaces – but also, more
by luck than judgement, I was there for a lot of them.
And made notes. Because what I saw of the facts
easily outstripped fiction.

Jim Fish: an insulting term for a black man; also used as a form of address.

Oxford Dictionary of South African English

Men will always be mad, and those who think they can cure them are the maddest of all.

Voltaire

CHAPTER I

Port Pallid, South Africa, 1984

In the mad middle years of the 1980s, in Port Pallid on the Indian Ocean, the old skipper of an inshore trawler, the *Lady Godiva*, was standing on the harbour wall one day, watching a line of leaping dolphins slicing through the waves, when he felt a tap on his shoulder.

'When I turned around,' he told Sergeant Arlow, 'there stood this boykie on the lip of the sea wall, looking at me with sea-green eyes. He might have come right up from the water, he was that close to it.'

'Better haul him in and let me see him,' said Sergeant Arlow, a great bear of a man, who decided all moral questions in Port Pallid. 'We will make a plan.'

The people of Port Pallid caught, thought, bought and sold fishes and weighed, sorted and grouped them into neat little piles; and they did much the same with people, adhering to the religion of Hendrik Frensch Verwoerd, a Dutch visionary who taught that people were happiest when coralled in separate ethnic enclosures, colour-coded for ease of identification and tightly controlled. All moral questions were matters for the police, and since Sergeant Arlow was the entire police force in Port Pallid it was he who decided to which group people belonged and whether their papers and passes and permits were in order.

And so the old skipper did as he was told, collected the boy and took him to the police station.

'Where you from, Jimfish?' the sergeant asked.

'When I was a baby I was stolen and taken away by some people to their village and worked as a slave in the fields,' the boy said.

'That's his story,' said the skipper.

'Believe that, you'll believe anything,' said the sergeant. He stuck a pencil into the boy's hair, as one did in those days, and waited to see if it stayed there or fell out before he gave his verdict.

'He's very odd, this Jimfish you've hauled in. If he's white he is not the right sort of white. But if he's black, who can say? We'll wait before classifying him. I'll give his age as eighteen and call him "Jimfish". Because he's a real fish out of water, this one is.'

The old skipper asked: 'What must I do with him?'

The sergeant shrugged. 'What would you do if you landed a catch the wrong size or colour?'

The skipper looked at the boy. 'I can't throw him back.'

'Put him on ice until his family comes forward,' said Sergeant Arlow. 'Until then, he can work in my garden.'

No one came forward to claim Jimfish and he remained impossible to classify. In some lights and to some eyes he looked as white as newly bleached canvas; others saw him as faintly pink or tan or honey-coloured; there were even some Pallidians who detected a faint blue tinge to the boy.

Jimfish lived in the house of the old skipper and each morning he waved goodbye when the *Lady Godiva* chugged into the Indian Ocean, heading for Cape Infanta, the Agulhas Bank or the Chalumna river mouth, chasing shallow-water hake or east-coast sole. When he returned from these trips the old skipper told the boy stories about strange creatures hauled up from the deep. One story above all others the boy asked for again and again.

'It was 1938 and I was a youngster like you, crewing on the trawler *Nerine* under Captain Goosen. One day we found in our nets this great big fellow. Blue as blazes with dabs of white. But this fish had four little legs. It turned out to be a coelacanth, which everyone thought had been dead for millions of years, but the one we caught was alive and kicking. The coelacanth can do handstands. And swim backwards. Folks say that humans come down from apes. But millions of years before that, Old Four Legs wandered ashore and decided to stay. Result? Us. And here we are, still fish out of water.'

Jimfish longed to join the fishing boats, but his permit allowed him to work only as a gardener. And so, when he felt sad, Jimfish would tell himself that even if he wasn't a proper person, and even if his family never came forward, one day he'd be a brother to this coelacanth.

'Bright blue, with four legs. It can stand on its head and swim backwards. A very queer fish. Like me.'

Each morning Jimfish went to work in the garden of Sergeant Arlow, whose wife Gloriosa kept on so many servants it was rumoured she assigned one to each hand when her fingernails needed attention.

Jimfish was set to work under the gardener, Soviet Malala, a most fiery man whose mother had been influenced by the Russian Revolution, hence the name she had given her son.

The Arlows had a lovely daughter, whose name was Lunamiel, and she had chestnut hair, green eyes and a complexion as soft as a downy peach. They had a son, too, named Deon, whose neck grew out of his collar like the trunk of a baobab and whose sole ambition was to become a policeman as large and loud as his father. It was also rumoured that even in starting a family Gloriosa had relied on a degree of in-house domestic help. But rumour-mongers were careful to keep their gossip from the ears of Sergeant Arlow, because policemen were encouraged to shoot troublemakers on a regular basis.

Soviet Malala felt sorry for young Jimfish and soon became the boy's teacher. This gardener, who had never been to school, taught himself to read and write. He studied the works of Karl Marx, Mikhail Bakunin and Kim Il-sung and then wove their ideas into his philosophy, which he named 'prolo-fisc-freedo-mism', and he explained its theories with boiling enthusiasm to his young apprentice.

'Anger ignites. It is the antidote to sickness, cynicism and doubt. Fury fires the masses and blasts them towards the right side of history. Rage is the rocket fuel of the lumpenproletariat.'

In this same year, 1984, a new, choleric, finger-wagging

4

president took charge of the country. He was known as 'Piet the Weapon', because of his passion for guns, tanks and fighter jets, and for crushing all who dissented, demurred or disagreed. When he one day paid a visit to Port Pallid, every white person turned out to hear him speak.

Spying an oddly coloured boy in the crowd, the President asked: 'And what's your group, young man?'

Jimfish did not hesitate: 'I'm with the fish, sir. That's my name and that's my calling.'

The President was impressed. 'Good for you, Jimfish. If we all stuck to our own school, shoal, tribe, troop and territory we'd be a lot happier. Those like Nelson Mandela, who oppose me, will stay in jail. There will be no mixing of the colours, no turning back and no going forward. In fact, no movement of any sort, not while I am in charge.'

The loyal Pallidians cheered him to the echo and felt very lucky to be led by a man so strong, so well-armed, so furious, and they sang him on his way:

> *Good old Piet, he's the one;*
> *We die for him till kingdom come;*
> *Given to us by God's own grace:*
> *Viva the champion of our race!*

And off went the new President to buy more weapons and do more crushing of anyone who dissented, demurred or disagreed.

'See what we are up against?' Soviet Malala asked his pupil. 'War is on the way. We will drive the colonial settler entity into the sea. Take back what he stole from us.

Confiscate his farms, reclaim the mines, nationalize the seas and abolish the banks. Viva the struggle! Viva the lumpenproletariat!'

When Jimfish said he wasn't sure if he qualified for the lumpenproletariat, his teacher told him: 'Think of the insulting name hung around your neck and you'll be as angry as a snake in no time at all.'

Jimfish promised to do his best and walked home longing to feel true rage, but knowing he was more fish than snake.

One day the *Lady Godiva* sailed back to port without its old skipper and Jimfish heard that he had been washed overboard. But in his dreams Jimfish saw the old man swimming with the coelacanth in deep-sea caves, where the two of them were doing handstands and paddling backwards. And he hoped that one day he could do the same.

He tried to tell Soviet Malala why he so loved the fish. 'It's bright blue, dabbed with white. It's got four legs and can stand on its head and swim backwards. A very queer fish. Like me.'

But the gardener shook his large head until his Lenin cap wobbled, and advised him to dream of revolution instead.

'When it happens we will nationalize the oceans and the fish will belong to formerly disadvantaged people like you.'

One afternoon Sergeant Arlow's daughter Lunamiel was walking in the orchard when she saw Soviet Malala sitting under a mulberry tree with one of her mother's maids, a vibrant girl named Fidelia, whose daily task it was to paint the fingernails of her mother's left hand. The gardener and the maid were so tightly entangled that Lunamiel, who loved botany, was reminded of the clutching tendrils of the strangler fig, but she had never seen two people in a such a binding embrace and she longed to try the experiment herself.

The very next day, after a long lesson from Soviet Malala on prolo-fisc-freedo-mism, Jimfish was walking through the sergeant's garden when he saw Lunamiel lazing on a red picnic rug beneath a mulberry tree. She asked Jimfish to sit beside her and he was happy to do so. Their hands touched, their breathing quickened, their clothing loosened, and soon Jimfish and Lunamiel were as tightly entangled as the tendrils of the strangler fig.

At that moment Sergeant Arlow came by, and when he saw the entangled two he pulled out his truncheon and began whacking Jimfish all over his body, much of which was exposed.

'You odd, foul fish!' he shouted. 'My daughter is as white as a wedding cake! Her family tree is Aryan to the nth degree!'

Lunamiel's mother, woken from her nap by the noise, overcame her exhaustion and marched into the garden, ready to give her daughter a good hiding, but she had forgotten which servant usually wielded the whip. Sergeant Arlow seized his service revolver to shoot the boy and Jimfish ran to Soviet Malala's room, where his teacher hid him under the bed until Sergeant Arlow, denied the chance of doing his duty, thrashed several of his servants instead.

Jimfish's relief did not last long. Soviet Malala warned

him it was only a matter of time before the sergeant shot
him and dragged his body behind his police van, a tradition among the constabulary. And if her father failed to kill
him, then Lunamiel's brother Deon was also very keen to
do so, having taken an oath on the family Bible that he
would never let his sister dally or tangle with a black man.

'I am not exactly black,' said Jimfish.

'You're not exactly anything and that's your trouble,' his
teacher pointed out. 'The best thing for you is to escape to
the outside world.'

Soviet Malala found a map and pointed to the country
north of the Limpopo river.

'Zimbabwe is the perfect place for you. Everyone is free,
happy and fed. Its leader is a true revolutionary and a
friend of Kim Il-sung of North Korea. He has done away
with imperialists and he will soon send the settler entity
packing. Zimbabwe is where South Africa will one day be.'

And so, that very night, Jimfish left Port Pallid on a long
march north. Every now and then he checked his temper-
ature, hoping to feel it flare into revolutionary rage, the
rocket fuel of the lumpenproletariat that blasts the masses
towards the right side of history.

CHAPTER 2

Zimbabwe, 1985–6

After walking for many weeks Jimfish reached the broad Limpopo river, on the far bank of which lay the country of Zimbabwe. He was weak and exhausted, but across the water he could see the outside world, and he silently saluted Soviet Malala for his escape, though he was unable to forget the lovely Lunamiel, left far behind in Port Pallid.

Some ferrymen, using rudimentary rafts of oil drums roped together, now offered to carry him to the other side of the river. Jimfish thanked them for their kindness, but said he would swim across.

'As you like,' they told him. 'But the water is full of crocodiles. They have eaten many refugees fleeing from the terror in Zimbabwe.'

'You are clearly mistaken,' Jimfish replied. 'I know for a fact – and my friend and mentor Soviet Malala has confirmed it – that across the Limpopo lies the land of the free, ruled by a kindly man, Robert Gabriel Mugabe, great friend of the eternal leader of North Korea Kim Il-sung, to whom all oppressed people look up, as living creatures look up to the sun.'

'If you believe that, you are in for a sad surprise,' said the ferrymen of the Limpopo. 'Then again, the ignorance of South Africans is limitless and legendary and nothing can help it. But if you truly wish to find out what lies across the river in Zimbabwe, you will need to arrive on the further bank without being eaten. For a modest sum we will carry you over.'

When Jimfish told them he had no money, the boatmen very kindly accepted his wristwatch in full and final payment, and, at nightfall, they paddled him across the Limpopo. The moment they deposited their passenger on the far bank they hurried back to the South African side of the river, as if their lives depended on it.

'How odd,' thought Jimfish, 'to wish to flee from the land of the free.' And he set off with a happy heart.

He had not gone far when a jeep packed with heavily armed soldiers wearing red berets drew up beside him.

'What are you doing on this road in broad daylight?' the soldiers demanded, astonished by Jimfish's lack of fear.

'I'm on my way to the capital where I hope to meet Robert Gabriel Mugabe, the Great Leader of this free land, comrade-in-arms of Kim Il-sung, dear leader of North Korea.'

'You're a lucky man,' the soldiers told him. 'We are the Red Division, a secret Zimbabwean force trained by those very same North Koreans to serve as the iron fist of our own great dear Comrade Leader. You are a most welcome volunteer to fight shoulder to shoulder with us against the filthy dissidents in this province of Matabeleland.'

Jimfish did not remember volunteering, but he was too polite to disagree when the soldiers pulled him into the jeep and drove him to their camp. There they fed him and gave him a bed and Jimfish was happy to be in a land where the colonialists had melted away, the settler entity would soon be no more, and the masses rejoiced in freedom and peace.

The next day he was shaken awake at dawn and sent on a route march of many miles to a rifle range where he was taught to use a gun, and then marched back to the camp, singing a revolutionary hymn, adapted from a Korean original:

> *Homage to Peasant Number One!*
> *Beloved Leader, bright Messiah,*
> *Whose holy light outshines the sun's;*
> *Whose eyes are lakes of liquid fire –*
> *Like rats his enemies succumb*
> *And roast upon their funeral pyre.*

When Jimfish asked who precisely was being honoured in this tribute, the soldiers explained it was the battle hymn of the Red Division, sung at sunrise, to honour either Kim Il-sung or the Great Leader of Zimbabwe. It did not matter which, since the two were interchangeable.

Before sunrise the next day, though grateful for his training, his food and his bed, Jimfish decided it was time to be on his way and left the camp quietly, not wanting to wake anyone. He had not gone far when a helicopter swooped low overhead, bullets peppered the red dust around him and he was arrested, manacled and flown back to the camp of the Red Division, where he was charged with desertion. Each day he was bound to a tree with barbed wire and whipped with electric flex until the flesh of his back ruptured. Then he was locked in one of the giant metal shipping containers that were used as classrooms or brothels or holding cells for suspected spies and dissident members of the Division.

Jimfish was dismayed by this treatment and knew he should be angry, but try as he might he could not feel revolutionary fury that was the rocket fuel of the lumpenproletariat. After some days, bruised, bleeding and close to dying of thirst, he asked his captors why he should be treated in this manner. They replied that he was lucky not to have been summarily shot. Instead, he was being reorientated, according to a method popular among the liberation movements of Southern Africa. If he survived re-education, he would join the ranks of the Red Division for their upcoming operation, dubbed 'The Storm that Drives the Rats from the Maize Fields'. Then they locked Jimfish in the shipping container again and left him to stew in the heat, flies and his own filth, while the Red Division went off to destroy a variety of villages across Matabeleland, whose inhabitants had failed to show proper respect for the Great Leader, brighter than the sun.

When the soldiers arrived back at the camp, after a day of rape and hut-burning, Jimfish told them that, rather than face another minute in the shipping container, he preferred to be shot. This they agreed to do, though they accused him of rank ingratitude. Jimfish was blindfolded and made to kneel. The firing squad had levelled their rifles when there rode by, in his regimental jeep, an officer built like a mahogany sideboard, his chest covered in golden medals and rainbows of ribbons.

'Who is this prisoner?' he demanded.

'A boy from south of the Limpopo,' the soldiers explained. 'He came in search of the sun itself, Kim Il-sung, of whom our Great Leader is the heavenly twin. But he failed to respond to reorientation.'

'Anyone south of the Limpopo, who is a champion of our own Comrade Leader in Harare, shows far more good sense than we ever expect from people down that way,' replied the officer. 'Release the prisoner immediately.'

The soldiers leaped to obey and Jimfish was taken to his saviour's ambulance, which followed him everywhere. There his wounds and abrasions were treated and, after many days of careful nursing, he recovered. His rescuer commended him for having the good sense to flee South Africa for the land of the free, and introduced himself.

'I am called General Jesus. Because I have the power to redeem or reject. I save or I damn. I am a military Messiah.'

The power of General Jesus was clear to see because his troops began treating their former prisoner with the utmost deference, commissioning Jimfish as an officer in the Red Division, placing on his head the prized red beret, and assuring him that any pain he might have felt when they beat him and locked him in the shipping container would soon be forgotten in the glory of hunting dissenters, rebels and traitors throughout the province of Matabeleland and bringing them the gift of correct reorientation. When Jimfish asked if there were dissidents who declined the gift, the soldiers were mightily amused at his simple-mindedness. Under the leadership of General Jesus, who took his orders directly from the Comrade President, only two classes of citizen were found in Matabeleland: the correctly reorientated and the recently deceased.

CHAPTER 3

Led – or rather, overseen – by the fearsome General Jesus, whose jeep followed at a sensible tactical distance, the Red Division advanced on the terrified villagers of Matabeleland. Men were few, and women and children scattered like chickens at the first glimpse of a red beret. What a splendid sight it is to see a full division of seasoned soldiers, armed with AK-47s, bayonets at the ready, trained in the Democratic Republic of North Korea, whose beloved leader dazzles like the sun, attacking a village of mud and thatch huts, with mortars, machine guns and rocket-propelled grenades.

When the soldiers tired of merely shooting people, they devised more recreational activities for passing the time. Jimfish watched as two pregnant girls were gunned down, soldiers slit open their bellies with bayonets and held up the still-living foetuses. Even though Jimfish pulled his beret over his eyes to block out the sight, nothing could muffle the screams of the dying girls.

Next, the survivors were interrogated and each was

asked to list his grievances regarding the actions of the Red Division. In the interests of transparency, General Jesus ordered that prisoners who refused to answer must have their grievances beaten out of them. Jimfish listened to a catalogue of rape, torture and the murder of family members carried out by the Red Division. But then all who claimed to have suffered these crimes were immediately ordered to deny it publicly. Next, the prisoners were given the Anthem of the Sun and made to sing the words:

> *You are the One*
> *Bright as the Sun;*
> *And we are thine*
> *From the start of time*
> *Till kingdom come!*
>
> *Who closes his eyes*
> *And blots out Our Sun;*
> *Deserves to die:*
> *By my machine gun!*

Once the interrogations and listing of grievances were done, the soldiers herded the prisoners into their huts, secured the doors and set fire to the thatch roofs. The screams of the burning men were such that Jimfish was again obliged to cover his ears as best he could with his red beret.

Being somewhat confused by what he saw, he approached General Jesus, who sat in his jeep watching the conflagration, and, apologizing for his ignorance, Jimfish asked: 'Is this cruelty intended to propel these villagers to anger and then to rage, which is the rocket fuel of the lumpenproletariat? In order that they rise and expel white colonial imperialist settler forces from the country?'

General Jesus smiled at his question. 'Those old bugbears were long ago booted out of Zimbabwe and we are free. Our leader in Harare is the choice of the people, and will be so until the last trumpet. But, alas, some in this province of Matabeleland refuse the hand of friendship and continue to harp on imaginary grievances. People here are tribalist, obstructionist and capitalist. Dissidents stalk the countryside. They must be firmly reoriented if they are to arrive on the right side of history.'

Hearing this, Jimfish felt a little happier because it reminded him of the words of his teacher Soviet Malala. But the air was so pungent with scorched flesh that he could not stop himself asking General Jesus: 'But what if some of those being burnt alive are already on the right side of history?'

The general smiled his jovial smile: 'We eradicate them anyway, because we can't say who is a dissident and who is not. History will know its own.'

The scene of suffering was too much for Jimfish (there is only so much you can mask with a red beret) and when the Division broke into a triumphal chorus of the national hymn – as the last huts and those trapped inside them burnt to ashes – Jimfish took the opportunity to slip away. Having walked for several hours through the bush he came to a village, which, from the tattered flag raised above the compound, he knew to be a loyalist community, linked by tribe and tradition to the faraway regime in the capital, Harare. Here was no smoke and no fire, but a deep and terrible silence. Arms, legs and heads lay scattered like broken dolls. In this village it had been the Matabele dissidents themselves who had fallen on the loyalists and hacked them to pieces, and the destruction was no less terrible than the one he had just fled.

As Jimfish lingered beside this field of carnage, debating in his heart whether any of these pitiful victims were on the right side of history, he was again taken prisoner by the Red Division, which had pursued him relentlessly since his escape. This time General Jesus was determined to show him no mercy.

Jimfish was imprisoned, along with dozens of Matabele prisoners whom the Brigade had rounded up – a crowd as thick as chaff on a threshing floor. They were made to stand on the banks of the nearby Cwele river and were summarily mown down with bursts of automatic fire. But so close was the press of bodies that, by a miracle, Jimfish was not touched, although he was buried under the weight of other victims and almost suffocated. He lay hidden until nightfall, when General Jesus ordered his troops to begin dumping the bodies down a nearby mineshaft. This was hard labour and the troops worked slowly; they complained about the weight of dead bodies, took frequent rest breaks and did not concentrate on their grisly work.

It was now that Jimfish again took the chance to escape. He walked through the night and the following day, thirsty, hungry and downhearted, knowing that the more distance he put between himself and his pursuers, the better was his chance of saving his life. He begged lifts from passing cars, and he was lucky to be picked up by a truck driver from Uganda, ferrying goods to the capital of Kampala, where, the driver told Jimfish, people were suffering terribly from army brutality and political stupidity.

'Our ex-President, Milton Obote, was an intellectual tyrant. He was chased away to make room for President Idi Amin. He was the boxer tyrant who enjoyed public executions. But he was chased away, too, and now we have Milton Obote all over again. He has an Academy where he gives people an education they never recover from – they graduate to the grave.'

The driver left him on a street corner in Kampala, where crowds were milling about. Some people were wildly happy; many were terrified and everyone was thin. When Jimfish asked what was going on, they told him there had been another coup and President Milton Obote had fled for a second time, taking with him all the money in the national bank.

'We have seen Idi Amin flee, only to be replaced by the dictator who came before him, Milton Obote. Now he has gone once again. Who is next? Is history a revolving door? Do despots always win? And, by the way, what tribe or species of creature are you? How is it that you are not white or black, neither man nor boy, fish nor fowl? Are you with us or against us?'

Jimfish had no answers to these question and he said simply: 'My name is Jimfish. I believe there is a right side of history and I hope one day to arrive there.'

This infuriated the crowd and they set the dogs on him

for being neither for nor against them, neither completely black nor sufficiently white but all the shades in-between, and Jimfish ran for his life. Sore and starving, he arrived on the edge of town and sat in the gutter beside a rubbish dump. An Asian gentleman named Jagdish saw his distress and took him home, gave him the run of his house, ran a bath for him, fitted him out with fresh clothes and set on the table a simple supper. When Jimfish thanked Jagdish for his kindness, the good man said he was sorry he could not do more. He had once been very rich, but the dictator before the dictator who had just fled had expelled all the Asians from Uganda. Most of his family had gone to England, but he had stayed and now he gave away what money he still had to those who had none.

'I am an African,' he said. 'I'm at home here in Uganda, and so I stay.'

Jimfish was very taken with this Asian who seemed not to care if he was on the wrong or right side of history, lacking the spark of anger that kindles the rage that is the rocket fuel of the lumpenproletariat. He stayed some days with the good Jagdish and when he had recovered with clean clothes on his back and some cash given him by his rescuer, he went to explore the town.

Beside the very rubbish dump where, not long before, he had sat down to beg, he saw another poor wretch, as thin as a flagpole and lying in the gutter, so deathly still that he might already have passed away. And in one hand he held what looked to Jimfish like a dried-out beetroot.

CHAPTER 4

Uganda, 1986

Remembering that he might have died in the self-same gutter had the good Jagdish not rescued him, Jimfish gave this beggar all the coins in his pocket. But when the poor man roused himself, seized his hand and tried to kiss it, Jimfish shook himself free, terrified of contagion.

'For heaven's sake!' said the beggar. 'Don't you recognize your friend and teacher Soviet Malala?'

Jimfish was amazed. His old mentor was so changed, even his Lenin cap had gone.

'What on earth has happened to you?' Jimfish said. 'The last time I saw you, in the garden of Sergeant Arlow, you were feisty and fit, ready to drive the settler entity into the sea. But here you are, a shivering wreck.'

'I think I'm about to faint,' said his teacher.

Gently Jimfish lifted him – he weighed no more than a bundle of firewood – and carried him back to the house of Jagdish, and there they fed and washed him and put him to bed. When Soviet Malala awoke, Jimfish was at his bedside.

'And now tell me,' he said, 'first of all, what has happened to the lovely Lunamiel?'

'Dead,' said the philosopher.

'Lunamiel dead?' Jimfish was devastated. 'Was it grief? Did she die heartbroken when I made my escape and left her?'

'Not at all,' Soviet Malala said. 'She was blown to bits in church one Sunday morning by a large bomb, timed to explode during the Communion. Many others in the congregation that day also died. Soon after you left Port Pallid the country descended into a low-grade civil war, with death squads of the white oppressor hunting down and killing black people, who resisted their tormentors and fought back with bombs and ambushes and riots. Which in turn led to further shootings by the reactionary settler entity of our revolutionary structures, cadres and formations. It was a time of frequent funerals and whoever caused the other side to bury more of their own, felt themselves to be winning the war. So as to be ready for freedom and the rise of the lumpenproletariat, I set off on a pilgrimage to the land that gave me my name, the Union of Soviet Socialist Republics, where everyone is equal, free, fed and fortunate. I followed your route and headed north.'

Jimfish felt he would be the next to faint, but managed a question: 'What has made you so thin and so ill? You who always swore that revolutionary anger was the antidote to sickness, cynicism and doubt, and that struggle forged sinews of steel?'

Now Soviet Malala looked desperately sad and Jimfish

had to bend closer to hear his whisper. 'Love. This is what love did to me.'

Jimfish remembered love and he had to agree that his own experience had not been altogether happy. 'I remember a barrage of blows from Sergeant Arlow's truncheon.'

'Painful, yet nothing compared with what I have suffered,' said Soviet Malala. 'Do you remember that plump young maid Fidelia, employed to paint the fingernails of Mrs Arlow's left hand? Well it was Fidelia, a sexual siren, who made love like one possessed and sent me into ecstasies of joy, who infected me with this deadly plague, which some call the 'slimmer's sickness'. She herself picked up this pox from a white farmer who used to visit her secretly, who got it from his black housekeeper, who got it from a Dutch Reformed pastor, who got it from the whore he visited every night, except on Sundays, who got it from a traveller in Central Africa, who, it is suspected, got it by transmission from gorillas or chimpanzees, eaten as bushmeat by people on the west coast of Africa. Or perhaps the route of this plague began in the European settler colonies, which imported reservoirs of cheap labour to build their railways and ports and roads. The Europeans worked their African labourers to death, but when replacements got too expensive they kept workers alive by inoculating them, often with unclean needles, against leprosy, yaws, syphilis and smallpox. Diseases which otherwise, and most mercifully, would have ended the miserable lives of their semi-slaves. However it started, the plague passed to me by the delightful Fidelia is beginning to rage across much of Southern Africa and it is yet another crime I lay at the door of the colonialists and imperialists.'

'A crime, certainly,' Jimfish agreed. 'But surely this disease must be fought or it will lay low the very militants who feel anger rising in them and turning to rage that fuels revolution. If the illness spreads it will kill the very structures, cadres and formations which you count on to expel the colonialists, imperialists and the settler entity.'

'Not at all,' said the philosopher of the lumpenproletariat. 'If we give our minds to the hidden agenda behind this slimmer's disease, we hear it said that the cause is a mysterious virus. It is the policy of our liberation movement to expose this assertion as a lie. It is further averred that the virus causes a syndrome that kills people. What nonsense! It is the very real diseases of Africa: TB, malaria, leprosy, malnutrition – these kill people. Not some fancy invention of western imperialists. This plague is a foreign plot, concocted in western laboratories for the express purpose of decimating the African continent, and South Africa in particular. Having first manufactured the illness, foreign drug companies offer drugs which will poison our people. It's a strategy aimed at the reconquest of Africa.'

'But if you don't seek treatment for this new plague, won't lots more people die?' asked Jimfish.

'Then dying will be our form of resistance,' Soviet Malala vowed. 'And as we do so, we will take comfort from the fact that the syndrome spreading across our continent will soon become our terrible export to our former colonizers. I predict they will soon begin dying in satisfactorily large numbers right across Western Europe and the United

States. Let them take their new drugs. But we will resist to the end.'

Jimfish was very confused: 'Then Africa is to be left with no defence against this sickness?'

'But, yes!' The philosopher reached beneath the bed-clothes and pulled out the dried beetroot he had been cradling when they met. 'If what I have is an African illness, then we must find traditional African remedies. The Central Committee of our movement has decreed that lemon juice, the African potato and beetroot will do the job far better than the poison of our enemies. Unfortunately, I had run out of money for food, I had sold even my old Lenin cap, sucked the lemon dry and polished off the potato and I was very close to finishing off the beetroot when you rescued me.'

Jimfish pointed out gently that although this treatment for his illness might have won Central Committee approval it had not helped him much.

'It may look that way to a non-Party member,' said Soviet Malala. 'But the beetroot-and-potato treatment is Party policy. And anyway, the new experimental drugs for treating the virus can be bought only from the United States and cost thousands of dollars and I am a poor man.'

That was enough for Jimfish, who went immediately to Jagdish and explained the matter to him. The good man picked up the phone and placed the order. 'What is the point of money if I don't help others?'

And so it was that the new drugs were flown at great expense from the United States, although Jimfish and Jagdish agreed that they would not mention this to Soviet

Malala. Once on the treatment, his viral load stabilized, he began to gain weight and he was in the happy position of claiming that he had been saved by the cocktail of beetroot, lemon juice and the native sweet potato. Now that he was well again his ambition to travel to the Soviet Union was keener than ever.

But Jagdish, who had travelled in Eastern Europe, was puzzled by this and quizzed Soviet Malala about his loyalty to Soviet Communism.

'I suppose you know that the USSR has some strange customs: there are separate schools for Party apparatchiks, separate lanes for their cars and separate privileges for the ruling caste. That sounds to me very like South Africa. Moreover, Soviet citizens are not well fed. The USSR and all its satellites never have enough bread to go around, nor shoes, socks, bathplugs or even toilet paper. And if its citizens are so fortunate, why do so many of them dream of running away?'

The philosopher was not to be budged. 'If there is a small degree of discomfort, it's so that citizens are always alert, pricked into the anger that fuels lumpenproletarian progress. If it were not so they might become so happy and peace-loving that their enemies would sweep over them.'

Jagdish agreed to buy air tickets and this turned out to be surprisingly easy because the new strong man of Uganda, who had just replaced Milton Obote, had decided that, after years of indigenous despotism, it was time to give the Soviet system free rein, and there were Russians all over Kampala selling arms and handing out the collected works of Marx, Engels and Lenin. Air tickets were soon bought and the three friends found themselves on a Soviet Aeroflot flight, bound for Moscow.

After the plane had left African airspace and begun its passage over Europe, Jagdish mused on the odd fact that, for a peace-loving people, the Soviets owned very many rockets capable of destroying the world.

Soviet Malala was quick to set him right: 'The missiles of the USSR are strictly for defence, unlike the arms of western imperialistic powers, which are intended to obliterate peace-loving people.'

As their plane crossed the Ukraine and they were nearing Kiev the sky darkened and far below they saw what looked like a sickly sun, pulsing among thick grey clouds. This was odd because it was long past midnight and the sun seemed very far below them. What could there be on the ground that might shine as brightly as the sun? Then the pilots of the plane announced to the passengers that they had been ordered to land. When Jagdish protested that they had paid to be flown to Moscow, the pilots retorted that it was from Moscow itself that the order had come.

Chapter 5

Chernobyl, Ukraine, 1986

The plane touched down at an airport called Zhulyany, which they were told was not far from Kiev. The good Jagdish, feeling sorry for Soviet Malala, so cruelly denied his first glimpse of Moscow, offered to buy him a ticket on another airline so that he might continue his journey.

The philosopher smiled at his ignorance, well-intentioned though it was.

'In the great Union of Soviet Socialist Republics there is only one airline, Aeroflot, just as there is only one political system, one party, one leader, one politburo and one right side of history.'

This gave Jimfish his chance to ask a question that had been worrying him since he had left Port Pallid: 'How will I know when I am on the right side of history? Who will I ask?'

Soviet Malala was happy to explain: 'There is no need to ask, no room for doubt, no chance of error. Just remember the central rule of Soviet socialism: everything not expressly permitted is always forbidden.'

Once on the ground, an elderly yellow coach drew up beside the aircraft and Soviet Malala said it was almost certainly a customary courtesy, this being doubtless the way in which the USSR welcomed all peace-loving visitors. The coach was packed with sleepy soldiers who would not give up their seats and the new arrivals had to stand in the aisle. Luckily, Soviet Malala, the son of a mother very much taken with the Bolshevik Revolution, had learnt Russian as a young child and he was ready to act as interpreter to his travelling companions. He asked the soldiers if they were on their way to a holiday camp, for in the Soviet Union workers enjoyed free vacations courtesy of the Communist Party.

This drew a surly response from a huge man with a great red beard, whose name was Ivan.

'Holiday? We are on our way to put out what the authorities tell us is a very minor fire. So small we will be back by nightfall, safe and sound. From this we surmise the blaze is so terrible nothing like it has been seen on earth before, a gigantic blaze burning out of control, and that few of us will return alive. We know this from the newspapers.'

Soviet Malala turned to his friends, delighted to say how open and informative were the newspapers in the Soviet Union. But the bearded giant told him he was talking nonsense.

'Our news services speak of disaster taking place somewhere else in the world. In the US or Canada or England. That's always a sure sign.'

'A sign of what?' Jimfish enquired.

'Of trouble at home. A dam has burst, an earthquake has

killed thousands, a submarine has sunk with all hands. When we are told this, we contact friends abroad to ask if they have news of a disaster in the USSR.'

Jimfish shook his head at this: 'If the Soviet Union is such an open, honest land why do its rulers lie to its citizens?'

'Because that's how it is,' said Ivan. 'They tell us next to nothing and we believe as little as possible.'

'How can a proud citizen of the socialist Motherland give way to such bitter cynicism?' Soviet Malala demanded. 'Aren't you proud of Marx, Lenin and Stalin?'

Ivan spat in the aisle where the travellers stood. 'Proud! If I were to visit the grave of Karl Marx in faraway London I would spit on it. If I bumped into Lenin I would stab him to death and dance on his corpse. As for Stalin, he murdered every member of my family and razed my village, and so I pray each night for his eternal damnation. From your stupid questions I know you are a fellow traveller, a foreigner and a fool.'

With that he pushed Soviet Malala to the floor and began to stamp on him as if he were Lenin himself. Luckily, his fellow soldiers pulled him off, pointing out that Soviet and his friends were volunteers and they needed all the volunteers they could find.

'But what on earth have we volunteered for?' Jimfish asked them.

The answer from the other passengers was a strange one.

'We are to be known as liquidators. All over the country thousands of liquidators are being mobilized to rectify what is said to be a minor technical mishap in a power station.'

'What is to be liquidated?' Jagdish wondered.

'Probably ourselves,' came the reply.

When, after a couple of hours, the bus came to a halt, they had arrived at a huge industrial plant or refinery topped by four large towers. From the mangled and blasted fourth tower flames were shooting hundreds of metres into the air. Now they understood that this must have been the glaring sickly sun they had seen from the sky. Helicopters hung above the flames constantly showering what looked like dust into the fires below, a scene which reminded Jimfish of children flinging handfuls of beach sand into the ocean.

'It's like hellfire,' said Jimfish.

'Not at all,' said Soviet Malala. 'It's a minor technical mishap. The Party will explain everything.'

Party apparatchiks took the volunteers into a briefing room, swore them to secrecy and told them about the minor mishap. There had occurred at Chernobyl nuclear power station an explosion that gave off many hundreds of times more radiation than the bomb the Americans had dropped on Hiroshima. The blast had blown the massive roof off Reactor Number 4, sending radioactive steam and dust high into the sky, and this cloud was, even now, floating over the USSR, heading west into Scandinavia, fanning out across most countries of Western Europe. Except, it seemed, for France, where the authorities insisted the radioactive cloud had either stopped at the country's borders or gone around the sides. Certainly, it had reached Great Britain, and Ireland and Canada were next in line. The toxic fallout from the blast had already tainted the lives of thousands, but the fear now was that a second explosion, much more powerful than the first, might occur at any time and trigger nuclear nightfall for millions. The Party line was to say little, admit nothing, and call for volunteers from all over the USSR to put out the flames. This would be their job as liquidators.

The soldiers whose bus Jimfish, Jagdish and Soviet Malala had joined were assigned to clearing the burning graphite debris from the roof of the stricken Reactor Number 4. Mechanical robots had been tried at first, but had broken down in the intense radiation pouring from the jagged hole. It was time to employ human technicians or 'bio-robots'. Each bio-robot was handed a gas mask, a hood, rubber boots and an apron thinly lined with lead. They were ordered to clamber up the iron staircases of the reactor, throw pieces of graphite off the roof, then run downstairs again as fast as possible. At no point should they remain on the roof for more than a few minutes.

'But why spend such a short time?' Jagdish asked.

The answer from the briefing officials was unusually detailed.

'While you are on the burning roof, you are directly exposed to high doses of radiation from caesium-137, strontium-90 and iodine-131. To stay there for more than a few minutes may somewhat damage your health. But great rewards await your patriotic heroism – all of you are in line for cash rewards, medals for bravery and the undying gratitude of the Motherland. Now put on your gear and report on the roof.'

The bio-robots in hoods and gas masks, wearing goggles that gave them the bug-eyed look of giant, white-eyed wasps, went clambering across the devastated roof, grabbing lumps of hot graphite and pitching them to the ground. The steam was so thick they could see very little. The huge soldier, Ivan, exhausted by heat and radiation, came very close to falling into one of the gaping fissures where the roof had split open and plunging into the searing depths of the reactor, and was saved only by Jagdish's quick action.

Not that his courage was appreciated.

'Why did you bother?' the giant snapped.

'Courage, comrade!' Soviet Malala cried. 'We are being tested in the fires of Party loyalty. And if we die, we will be heroes of the Motherland, third class.'

'Shut your face,' was Big Ivan's angry reply, 'or I will pitch you head first into the inferno at the heart of this reactor. Our lives are over anyway, none of us has a chance.'

The next day it was Jagdish who collapsed on the rooftop and – as Jimfish watched, horrified – Big Ivan bent over him, rifled through his pockets, removed his wallet and, without a second thought, tipped him as if he were no more than a sack of coal into the jagged hole where the fuel rods pulsed in the eerie blue water.

When Jimfish shouted out in horror at what he had seen, Big Ivan merely flourished Jagdish's wallet and announced: 'To each according to his needs.'

Then he clambered down the ladder and made off,

closely followed by Jimfish and Soviet Malala, who ran clumsily in their heavy hoods, masks and lead-lined aprons, shouting, 'Stop, thief!' and looking for all the world to the liquidators who watched the chase from the roof of the reactor like actors in some antique black-and-white film.

CHAPTER 6

Pripyat, Ukraine, 1986

Jimfish and Soviet Malala followed Ivan to the nearby town of Pripyat, where an enormous street party of thousands of revellers was in progress, and in the melee of marching bands, choirs and fair-ground fun, they lost their man. Jimfish turned in some perplexity to his friend and mentor.

'Surely this is no time for a party? That reactor could explode a second time and destroy much of Europe.'

'Today is the First of May,' Soviet patiently explained. 'And on May Day everyone in the Motherland celebrates the triumphant workers of the Soviet Union. Nothing could be more natural.'

Jimfish pondered the crowds dancing in the streets: 'Chernobyl is close by and these people celebrating here in Pripyat don't even have lead-lined aprons. They're taking in so much radiation it will kill them.'

'All the more reason for a good party – if things are as bad as that, which I doubt, they will die happy,' Soviet assured him. 'What we face at Chernobyl is certainly a technical challenge, but we must trust the Party to think of a way. Finding Ivan will not be hard. He's an assassin who has insulted the Motherland and sold his Soviet citizenship for the dollars in poor Jagdish's purse. He'll have headed for some place he can spend the money and there aren't many of those. We must track him down and denounce him to the authorities, who will certainly send him to a labour camp.'

And he was right. They found the absconding soldier in the best restaurant in Pripyat, on the corner of Lenin Avenue and International Friendship Street, eating sturgeon and knocking back vodka. In between bites of fish and swigs of vodka, he was singing a popular Soviet song: 'We were born to make fairy tales a reality . . .'

Except, as Soviet explained somewhat testily to Jimfish, instead of *skaska*, the Russian word for 'fairy tale', Ivan used a shocking pun, and his song now went: 'We were born to make *Kafka* a reality.'

When the two friends challenged Ivan and demanded he hand back Jagdish's wallet, he laughed, opened another bottle of vodka and told them to get lost. 'I've done you a big favour. If you had stayed up on the roof of the reactor, you'd be goners. Just like all these fools marching and dancing in the streets of Pripyat.'

'Why have this May Day parade if Pripyat is a death zone?' Soviet demanded.

'Because it diverts attention from the horrible reality of things,' said Ivan. 'The May Day charade is the purest summation there can be of how things are done here. Today the party, tomorrow the death march. Hundreds of thousands of people will be moved out of Pripyat; the fair-ground will stand empty, the swimming pools deserted, the children's swings in the parks will rust and no one will ever be allowed back.'

Big Ivan had no sooner said this, while continuing to guzzle his sturgeon, when Jimfish began to feel nauseous; soon he was vomiting, then he had a feverish headache and sat down, overcome by dizziness.

'Help me – I am not myself,' he implored.

'All very typical symptoms of radiation sickness. Your fishy friend will almost certainly kick the bucket,' Big Ivan told Soviet Malala, taking a gulp of vodka. 'He's better off dying here than on the roof of Reactor Number 4. You know how this will be handled if ever we put the fire out. At the end of the day the bio-robots still standing will be thanked, presented with 100 rubles and a big medal and be sent home to die. That won't be the end of it. They'll have to be buried in lead-lined coffins, because their bodies will be radioactive for many thousands of years. Like Chernobyl itself.'

'It is inconceivable that heroes of the Soviet Union should perish, having done everything to save the Motherland,' Soviet Malala said firmly. 'The Party would never allow it.'

Big Ivan laughed: 'On the contrary. The patriotic duty of a liquidator is, precisely, to liquidate himself, as your friend is now doing. The fewer witnesses there are to this catastrophe, then so much the better. That's why our rulers fiddle while Chernobyl burns. Here we see the worst nuclear accident of our times, a deadly danger to millions, from Iceland to America and yet, to read our papers, you'd believe nothing has happened.'

'That is not true,' said Soviet Malala, seizing a copy of the newspaper *Pravda* from a nearby table. 'Look at this paragraph on page three: "Small mishap at Chernobyl, now under control."'

'You are either a madman or a devil,' Big Ivan told him. 'The radioactive cloud from Reactor Number 4 – in the middle of which we ridiculous bio-robots worked so recently – is now wafting across the globe, poisoning whatever it touches.'

'Ah, that goes to show the immense moral gulf between the US and the USSR,' said Soviet Malala. 'When a nuclear reactor leaked radioactivity into the atmosphere in New York a few years ago the authorities tracked the fallout in America meticulously, but they were blind to the damage in other countries. The USSR alone develops the peaceful atom and shares it with the whole world.'

'At least the US plans to murder its enemies with its nuclear weapons,' said Big Ivan, 'but the Soviet Union kills its own citizens at Chernobyl and says nothing about it.'

Then he paid for his lunch from Jagdish's wallet, handed the waitress a large tip, put his arm around her waist and they headed upstairs.

'Where are you going?' Soviet Malala followed him, but Ivan simply picked him up and threw him into the stairwell, saying as he did so, 'I have a full belly, a head nicely addled with vodka, dollars in my pocket and I'm on my way to bed with a willing waitress: things I have prayed for all my life have come to me now in this ruined city.'

'Courtesy of the good Jagdish.' Soviet Malala spoke from the bottom of the stairwell.

'He was better than good!' Big Ivan roared. 'He made a Russian happy! He was a saint!' And he vanished into a bedroom with the willing waitress.

'For heaven's sake, get me a doctor!' Jimfish begged.

But the joyous music of the May Day bands and the hubbub of happy children drowned his words and Jimfish passed out in the corner of the restaurant.

There he may have died, but luckily the waiters in the restaurant had alerted the KGB to the presence of two strangers, one of whom was black and the other too many different shades of colour to be safe. The black man, they reported, had been spreading all sorts of ridiculous lies about the Soviet Union.

When the police arrived and arrested him, Soviet protested his great love for the USSR, his reverence for Lenin, Stalin, Khrushchev, Brezhnev, Gorbachev and Soviet Atoms for Peace. It was clear to everyone that this man understood nothing whatever about life in the Soviet Union and must be a foreign spy. So, indeed, was his pallid companion, except he seemed to know nothing at all about anything. The authorities decided that it made sense to shoot the black spy, since he was surely of far less importance than his paler partner. So it was that Soviet Malala was taken out into the town square, a firing party of soldiers from the May Day parade, very much the worse for vodka, was hastily assembled and, after several botched attempts, the poor philosopher was shot.

This spectacle greatly cheered the spectators, which was

just as well, for it was the last enjoyment they were to have. At the end of the May Day party dozens of yellow coaches – like the one that had met their plane when Jimfish, Soviet and Jagdish arrived at Kiev Airport – drew up and, under the watchful eye of armed soldiers, tens of thousands of people were removed from their city; then farm animals and domestic pets were shot, farmhouses were dynamited, guards were posted on roads and bridges to ensure that no one returned, and the city of Pripyat was closed for ever.

CHAPTER 7

Moscow/Perm, 1987–9

Jimfish knew he might have died in Pripyat; perhaps he *should* have died, whether by firing squad or of radiation sickness like many bio-robots of Chernobyl. He had seen the good Jagdish cruelly killed by Big Ivan, whose life he had saved; he had watched his mentor Soviet Malala clumsily executed by a drunken firing squad. Yet for reasons he did not understand his life was spared and he had been flown – on the very plane in which he had arrived in Kiev – to Hospital Number 6 in Moscow, the sole establishment capable of dealing with severe cases of radiation sickness.

Thanks to special treatment his symptoms abated. The effects might resurface in years to come, he was told by the doctors, but for now he was fine. When Jimfish thanked the medical staff for their care, they replied that his brave work as a bio-robot on the roof of the ruined reactor at Chernobyl had won their admiration, even if they felt a certain regret that, having helped to save his life, he was to be transported to a distant penal colony as an American spy.

'But I'm not a spy!' Jimfish cried. 'I am not even American. I come from a little town called Port Pallid in South Africa.'

But none of the doctors at Hospital Number 6 had the vaguest idea where South Africa was – and even if this were true, they asked, why was he not black?

The secret camp to which he was sent was known as Perm 35, one of a constellation of jails, mental asylums and penal colonies a thousand miles east of Moscow. It was a 'special' prison for 'special' prisoners, one of a type which the authorities claimed had been closed down, and so it did not officially exist. Row upon row of desolate wooden barracks where the huts were furnaces in summer and iceboxes in the snow, and the guards were paid extra well to see to it that prisoners never escaped. In any case, it would have been hopeless to have done so, because beyond Perm 35 stretched endless, empty forests.

Jimfish was happy to discover that many of his fellow prisoners were poets and philosophers; gentle people who helped him to learn some Russian and who talked about openness, renewal, liberty and love, much as they had been doing before they were arrested and sent to Perm 35. What he found hard to fathom was why they had been locked up for such talk. What would his old teacher Soviet Malala have said about this?

'Obviously the Party in Moscow has made a mistake,' Jimfish decided, 'and as soon as this is corrected, we will be freed.'

His fellow prisoners were at first amused, then alarmed by a man so secure in his ignorance, so quick to take moral positions, so blind to what was in front of his nose that he must be a holy fool, a lunatic or even an American, as the authorities in Moscow had charged.

Jimfish had spent a couple of years in Perm 35 when one day without warning he was freed from his cell, driven to an airport and placed on a plane, which took off for an undisclosed destination. It was November, snow was falling and, looking down upon the vastness of Russia below him, he wept when he recalled the fate of Jagdish, dead in Reactor Number 4, and Soviet Malala, shot for all the wrong reasons in the ghost city of Pripyat.

Some hours later the plane circled above a city seemingly cut in half by what looked like a long wall, but he had no idea where he might be. Only when he had been securely locked in a new prison cell did an officer from State Security (its motto: 'The Sword and Shield of the Party') inform him that he was in Berlin, a guest of the German Democratic Republic. As an important American spy he would be exchanged for an important Soviet agent. A few days later the same man from the Stasi took him to a place called Checkpoint Charlie to rehearse the coming exchange. Curious, as always, about the traditions of foreigners, Jimfish asked him about the long dividing wall he had seen from the air.

'It is not a wall,' the Stasi officer told him. 'We never use that word. What you see is an anti-fascist protection rampart running for a hundred miles, consisting of concrete, wire mesh, trenches, fences, mines, listening devices, dogs and armed guards.'

'Is it there to keep people in or out?' Jimfish asked.

'It's there to protect us from the subversion and aggression of those on the western side of the rampart, and thus on the wrong side of history,' came the reply. 'The guards are ordered to shoot anyone silly enough to try crossing to the other side.'

From which Jimfish concluded that anyone even glancing across the rampart was already on the wrong side of history.'

The Stasi officer agreed. 'Being wedded to the purest form of socialism, we occupy that point where history ends; we are its culmination and its apotheosis. In other words, the right side of history is us.'

Jimfish was deeply impressed and longed for the day when he would be closer to that point himself.

His cell included a small television set on which he saw, day after day, political speakers addressing large crowds in the streets. None of it did he understand, but he took it that the speakers were assuring the crowds that they were wedded to the purest form of socialism, as well as being the culmination of history. But the crowds seemed to listen less and less and took to climbing the anti-fascist protection rampart and riding on it, as if they were children and it were a nursery rocking horse instead of a concrete barrier many miles long, bristling with guards, dogs and barbed wire. Next, the climbers began chipping away at the anti-fascist protection rampart, using hammers and chisels, and no one came to stop them. It was all very puzzling.

At night Jimfish lay in his cell listening to chisels chinking on concrete, as if legions of steel-beaked woodpeckers were chipping to bits the anti-fascist protection barrier.

Soon there were large holes everywhere and people walked through these gaps, helped by the very guards who, just days earlier, were ready to shoot anyone who did this.

Jimfish's TV screen began showing pictures of whole families of East Germans clambering though holes in the barrier and heading into western Berlin, stopping to stare for long minutes at cakes and shoes and pickles in the bright windows of the supermarkets, or wandering down Martin-Luther Strasse, awestruck by billboards advertising 'Big Sexy Land'. If the western side of the barrier was on the wrong side of history, why did these people want to go there?

Jimfish wished he could have talked this over with his mentor Soviet Malala: surely he would have known why the world seemed so suddenly to have been stood on its head; why the barrier had great holes in it and why State Security headquarters, where he had been locked up, had gone so very quiet. It was the strangest feeling: his prison, a hubbub of clanging cell doors and shouted orders, was suddenly as silent as the grave.

CHAPTER 8

East Berlin, 1989

When Jimfish tried his cell door, it was unlocked and he wandered at will in the deserted building, lights left burning, filing cabinets open, office after office knee-deep in ribbons of shredded paper, as if someone had wanted to destroy as many files as possible. When he walked outside he was swept up in crowds chanting *'Wir sind eine volk!'*, which, as he spoke Afrikaans, he understood to mean 'We are one people!' But why should they insist on it? he wondered. What else could they be?

Jimfish shouldered his way through the jubilant throngs, left the deserted Stasi Headquarters and walked to the once-imposing Protection Rampart, now torn by gaping holes. A smiling border guard happily helped him to clamber through a gap into the western side of town, where an official greeted him with an envelope stuffed with a hundred German marks. Jimfish understood not a word but his benefactor's demeanour told him that the cash was 'welcome money', a gift to spend in the gigantic street-party that engulfed Berlin. So it was that each day he joined the joyous, tipsy crowds carousing from Karl-Marx-Allee in the East to the Kurfürstendamm in the West, returning in the evening to sleep in his old cell at Stasi Headquarters, barely aware of the days flying by. Before he knew it, November had gone and with it all but the last *pfennigs* from his stash of welcome money. From what he had seen of the heart of newly unified Berlin, Jimfish felt that the welcome cooled as his money dried up, and he knew he would have to move on.

One evening in the midst of the singing, dancing, ecstatic tumult, Jimfish noticed a small man, well muffled against the winter cold, wearing a black conical astrakhan hat. He seemed alarmed by the fierce joy of the crowds, shaking his head and repeating again and again: 'It's time to change, it's time to change.'

'What? Do you mean the way this country is run?' Jimfish asked him.

'No, no,' said the little man. 'This is not change. It's anarchy. I mean it's time for me to change my clothes and have them burnt. I have done so every morning all my life. But my staff deserted me to gape at this hysterical rabble and I've not put on a clean suit for days.'

'But why burn your suit after wearing it just once?' Jimfish asked.

'To protect myself against radioactive contamination. Even when I went to visit the Queen in Buckingham Palace in London I took a fresh suit for each day, as well as my own sheets. Her Majesty made me a Knight Grand

47

Cross of the Most Honourable Order of the Bath, but I'd give my knighthood away right now for a fresh change of clothes. And a shower.'

'Well, if it's contamination that worries you, then steer clear of me,' warned Jimfish. 'I've spent time in Chernobyl putting out the fire and my radioactive reading is probably off the scale.'

'If you've been in the Soviet Union then yours will be socialist radiation from the peaceful atom. And it is to a semblance of socialist order that I must return very soon. Do you happen to know what Lenin said in 1903?'

Jimfish had to confess he did not.

'He said: "Where one or two socialists are gathered, there the glass must be raised." From which part of the world are you?'

'Africa,' said Jimfish.

'I have a great friend in Africa. He runs Libya and comes to visit us often. We are brothers under the skin. He is called "The Guide" and I am "The Genius of the Carpathians" or, if you prefer, the "Danube of Thought". As a socialist you should get out of this country right now before you catch whatever contagion is on the loose and go back to Africa.'

'That's not possible. I have nothing. No money and no transport,' Jimfish confessed.

'Then come with me,' said the little man in the black conical hat who burnt his suits each day. 'I have a helicopter waiting.'

He hurried Jimfish into a huge palace, ablaze with light. 'This is, or was, the home of my old friend Erich, the ruler

48

of the German Democratic Republic, until he made an unfortunate series of missteps.'

Jimfish gazed at the blazing forests of chandeliers, neon and fairy lights that lit up the vast palace, admiring especially the veritable zoo of stuffed animal heads everywhere on the walls.

'He owns a lot of lights, your friend.'

The Genius of the Carpathians nodded. 'This palace is known to locals as "Erich's Lamp Shop", because he can afford so many lights and everyone else must make do with a few weak bulbs.'

Jimfish could not help smiling and before he could compose his face, the little man frowned.

'Allowing jokes was just one of Erich's missteps. The other mistake was his wall.'

'You mean putting it up?' Jimfish asked.

'Not at all.' The little man shook his head so vigorously his conical hat almost flew off. 'His mistake was to let it fall. This is a leader who said, just the other day, that his wall will be standing in fifty or a hundred years. But as you have seen, it is being pulled down before our eyes, without so much as a by your leave! The guards who yesterday were primed to shoot escapees are today helping little old ladies to scrabble through the cracks and claim their one hundred marks welcome money from the West Germans, then head out to shop in the Kurfürstendamm. It's disgusting! Let's leave this failed state before we are polluted.'

'Shall we switch off some of these lights first?' Jimfish asked. 'Or Erich will face a very large electricity bill when he gets home.'

'He's unlikely to be back this way,' said the little man. 'He left a few hours ago for Moscow. Now follow me.' He led the way down some stairs and into a secret tunnel. 'This is an emergency route Erich built in case he ever needed to leave quickly and quietly.'

The Genius of the Carpathians and Jimfish hurried along the tunnel beneath Erich's Lamp Shop, passing under the Schlossplatz, and came out in what had once been the stables of the German emperor on the banks of the Spree river. And here a helicopter was waiting, its rotors whirling.

CHAPTER 9

Bucharest, Romania, 1989

As the helicopter rose, Jimfish could see below him
the wall that once divided the city pocked and perforated
by the iron beaks of hundreds of human woodpeckers.
The Genius of the Carpathians sat beside him, rehearsing
a speech he was to make as soon as he arrived home.

'There has been a little bit of difficulty in my country.
Doubtless encouraged by the appalling events of the falling wall in Berlin. Instead of doing the decent thing and
sending in the tanks, our Russian friends have been
unhelpful. They keep talking about what they call "openness" and "reconstruction". This is madness. As my old
comrade Kim Il-sung likes to say, "The openness we need
is found in the barrel of the gun." And as for "reconstruction", that's for reactionaries. We true Communists prefer
cementation. Provocation must be crushed.'

The pilot of the helicopter was on the radio and told his
chief what he was hearing: 'It's more than provocation, sir.
It's wholesale insurrection in Timişoara and Bucharest.'

The little man was having none of it. 'As soon as we

touch down in my capital, I will address the cadres, structures, formations and Party elements and all dissenters will be obliterated.' And then, looking down from a great height on his capital city, he formally welcomed Jimfish to the Socialist Republic of Romania.

'I feel I have built the place myself.'

As the chopper dropped lower, Jimfish could make out among the huge buildings tiny, ragged creatures wheeling sticks of firewood along icy boulevards. When he remarked on how lone and lost they looked, the little man in the conical astrakhan hat smiled at his ignorance.

'Those are individuals and do not count. Only the masses have weight. When we speak, thousands are wheeled out to applaud and then loosed against the provocateurs. Wait and see.'

As they prepared to land he pointed to various landmarks. 'You can see the Palace of the People, a monument to the Party and the masses, inspired by a similar marvel erected by my friend Kim Il-sung, that pharaoh amongst pygmies. But mine is larger.'

Jimfish said he had never in his life seen anything so big.

The Genius of the Carpathians nodded so happily his conical astrakhan hat wobbled. 'I wanted it to be seen from outer space. To build it, we first knocked down most of the old historical centre of Bucharest, along with a couple of dozen churches, six synagogues and got rid of no fewer than thirty thousand houses.'

'Why did you do that?' Jimfish asked.

His friend smiled. 'My capital city was once known as

Little Paris. But I came, I demolished, I redeveloped. And Little Paris became Big Bucharest.'

The helicopter put down on the roof of a tall building that his friend identified as his home from home, the Central Committee of the Communist Party. Waiting to greet them were army officers, policemen, bodyguards and important Party officials in big caps with huge peaks and Jimfish began to appreciate how special his new friend was. Whenever he spoke, everyone in hats clapped in unison and took up the chant: 'Ni-co-lae Cea-oooo-şes-cooo . . . . Romaneeeeaaah!'

Among the welcoming party was a stern woman and she now called out to the Danube of Thought: 'For heaven's sake, Nicolae! You look like a tramp. I can see you haven't changed your clothes in days.'

Whereupon the little man turned pale and went into a huddle of security men, in a manner Jimfish had seen on a rugby field, when a player wished to replace his torn shorts in a modest manner. When he emerged he wore a new suit, although whether his astrakhan hat had been replaced Jimfish could not tell.

'Now burn the old suit,' ordered the stern woman. 'It's sure to be infected with Falling Wall syndrome.'

Just how important she was Jimfish understood when his friend introduced her: 'This is Lenuţa, Deputy Prime Minister, Mother of the Nation, Head of the Cadres Commission, Revolutionary Fighter for the Motherland, as well as being my wife.'

Lenuţa straightened Nicolae's conical hat, fussed with his scarf, buttoned his winter coat, and Jimfish was invited to accompany the presidential couple, police officers, body-guards and bulky Securitate agents to the balcony overlooking the gigantic square, where thousands waited in the December chill. Even though Nicolae had been rehearsing his speech on the helicopter, he was slow in getting started and mumbled a lot.

The Deputy Prime Minister kept hissing at her husband, 'Speak up, Nicolae!'

The helicopter pilot interpreted Nicolae's remarks for Jimfish, who got the impression that depite rehearsing his speech, Nicolae was floundering. He spent long minutes greeting the municipal workers, soldiers and city councillors. The crowd muttered and hissed and, although some factory workers clapped, rattling their banners in support, the muttering and hissing in the square grew noisier as Nicolae sputtered on. Suddenly, a series of explosions that might have been fireworks or even gunshots were clearly audible. Nicolae became very irritated and banged the microphone, shouting 'Halloo! Halloo!' in the manner of a schoolmaster chivvying his pupils. Then there began a sound no one had heard in decades, when the Genius of the Carpathians addressed the nation: a hullabaloo so brazen and impudent that everyone on the presidential balcony refused to believe what their ears told them.

'Surely it's the wind wafting your achievements to the world,' said a Securitate officer.

'Or a choir of owls saluting the greatness of your genius,' said a second man.

These artful attempts to explain the angry booing that interrupted Nicolae's speech from the balcony were received in silence by the Genius of the Carpathians.

Lenuţa knew instantly that something alarming was happening, and shouted, 'Speak to them, Nicolae!'

In the pandemonium, her orders seemed to Jimfish as fruitless as the helicopters he'd watched sprinkling sand on the flames of the Chernobyl reactors. The leader's body-guards now decided it was time to put a good deal of space between themselves and the mob.

A Securitate man dared to interrupt the leader. Sidling up to him, he tapped Nicolae on the shoulder: 'We could use the tunnels below the square, which you, sir, had the foresight to build.'

The Danube of Thought shook his conical hat. 'That way we'll end up in the middle of these madmen, like moles coming up in the neighbour's garden; they'll reach for a spade and smash our heads in. Better we take the helicopter to a friendly barracks, return in force with loyal soldiers, then shoot everyone who opens his mouth.'

The functionaries on the balcony agreed this was a sound idea and hurried the presidential couple into the lift and up to the roof of the Palace of the People, while far below the angry mass in the square surged around the walls of Party Headquarters like a wild sea.

Perhaps he had come at last, Jimfish realized, face to face with the rage of the lumpenproletariat. Yet how could this be, in a land devoted to the health and happiness of just that favoured class whose champion was Nicolae Ceauşescu and whose side he was on? If history had so very many sides, however would he know the right one?

CHAPTER 10

Târgoviște, Romania, December 1989

The helicopter was lifting when Nicolae's wife suddenly remembered something she had forgotten.

'We can't go without the gifts. And fresh changes of suits for Nicolae.'

So lift-off was aborted and into the strong room ran the presidential couple, and the safes were opened. Lenuța had been referring to the official gifts with which Nicolae had been presented by many heads of state over his twenty-five years in power: leopard skins from Mobutu Sese Seko of Zaire; silver doves from the Shah of Persia; an enamelled yak from Mao Zedong; portraits of Lenin and Stalin; and even a bullet-proof limousine.

But the crowds downstairs had now broken into the building and were heading for the roof. Though Lenuța sighed at having to leave behind shoals of shoes, forests of furs and towers of tiaras, she snatched the diamonds given to her by Jean-Bédel Bokassa, then ruler of the one-time Central African Empire. Her husband took only the moon rocks presented to him by the American President Richard

Nixon, stuffing them into his pockets, before the Securitate officers, hearing the shouts of their pursuers who were now racing up the stairs, pushed the presidential couple into the lift, which creaked and trembled as it climbed, under the combined weight of the bodyguards, then broke down on the top floor and the doors had to be forced open. By now, so terrified were Nicolae and Lenuţa, they had to be half-carried to the waiting helicopter.

Nicolae seemed to regard Jimfish as a lucky token, because he insisted he come with them. Two bodyguards climbed aboard, which meant Lenuţa had to perch un-comfortably on Jimfish's knee. But there was no time for objections; the first demonstrators were on the roof, heading for the helicopter as it lifted.

Nicolae was elated, swearing to return with troops loyal to him and to the cause. But not long into the flight, the pilot announced that they were being tracked by radar and could be blown out of the sky at any moment.

'Then put down immediately!' Nicolae ordered, seeing a road beneath them.

As soon as they touched down, one of the Securitate men leaped out and stopped a passing car, showing his pistol by way of encouragement as he ordered the aston-ished driver to accept several passengers. But in the tiny car they were even more crowded than they had been in the helicopter and Nicolae was obliged to jettison his body-guards.

It was in these cramped conditions that they arrived in a town called Târgovişte and found a house where the owner showed them to a room and promised they would be safe. Lenuța was wary and cautioned Nicolae with a Romanian proverb she translated for Jimfish: 'Do not sell the skin till you have shot the bear.' But her husband ignored her.

Once the presidential couple were inside the room, Jimfish was relieved to see the owner of the house turn the key in the lock, sure that this was done to protect them. It was only when he heard Nicolae banging on the door and a troop of soldiers suddenly arrived and took up guard outside the room that Jimfish realized something was amiss.

'What are you doing here?' he asked the soldiers.

But they did not understand him. However, the pilot who had announced to his boss – falsely it seemed – that their helicopter could be blown out of the sky at any moment, suddenly reappeared. He translated Jimfish's question for the soldiers, who were most amused and gave this answer: 'We are here to shoot the dictator and his wife.'

'Without a trial?' Jimfish was shocked.

'Of course there is to be a trial. The dictator and his wife will be charged with treason, fraud, murder and embezzlement. When found guilty they will be executed.'

Jimfish felt more confused than ever. 'But then this is not a revolution, it's a military coup.'

'You're a simple lad,' the soldiers told him, 'and you can't see the difference between a coup and a revolution. Where have you been all your life?'

'I come from Africa,' Jimfish told them.

'Ah, well,' they nodded, 'that explains it. In Africa you

have a coup every day of the week. That's to say a violent, undemocratic takeover of the state, often by disaffected military men. Our revolution is very different. It's a spontaneous democratic uprising, led by and for the people. Anyone who calls it a coup is a counter-revolutionary simpleton and will face the same fate as the dictator, if this simpleton is not careful.'

Jimfish still failed to see the difference, though he was too polite to say so. He was keenly reminded of his own country, where show trials, run by supine judges, reduced legal tribunals to loyal mouthpieces of the regime and turned judicial chambers into kangaroo courts. His puzzlement must have been clear to the soldiers, who were gripped by a burst of missionary desire to enlighten this benighted African. When Jimfish offered to leave the house, they insisted he stay and see how much better things were done in Europe. So it was that Jimfish had a seat at the events that now unfolded.

First, the soldiers drew lots as to which of them would serve in the firing squad. Then they selected the wall against which the guilty pair would be shot the moment their trial ended. Next the haggard defendants were led into the courtroom to face the military judges. A lawyer, brought from Budapest to represent the prisoners, advised them to tell the court they were mad. Nicolae refused to recognize the legitimacy of the court, while Lenuţa – who was, it seemed, more widely known as Elena – said little.

Arriving at the verdict took no time at all.

Jimfish watched as the condemned prisoners were bound with rope and marched to the appointed wall. The firing squad took a few steps back and then, apparently unable to wait another moment, the soldiers wheeled, opened fire and kept shooting. Other soldiers appeared at upstairs windows and joined in the fusillade, so that, for long moments after the first shots knocked Nicolae and Elena to the ground, dozens more bullets continued to buffet their bodies, making them shake and quiver as if alive.

Finally, silence settled and the bodies were carried away to be buried in unmarked graves. All those who had taken part in the execution wished each other a very happy Christmas and said it was the best gift they could have had. Jimfish briefly wondered if he should have said something about the diamonds of the Emperor Bokassa, which Elena had in her pocket, or the moon rocks from Richard Nixon that Nicolae carried, but he rather feared the soldiers would immediately dig up the bodies again.

Terrible though the scenes had been, he tried to feel grateful for being shown why a military coup was not to be confused with a revolution, and exactly where a fair trial differed from a kangaroo court. But the knowledge was bitter. He had begun to see that such things depended on a triad of useful principles: first – on who had the guns; next on who was dead when the shooting stopped; and last but most important: on who was in charge of the words used to talk about what had happened when it was all over.

CHAPTER II

Bucharest, Romania, Christmas 1989

Jimfish flew back to Bucharest, on Christmas Day, aboard the same helicopter in which he had begun his journey with Nicolae and Lenuţa-Elena. He landed once again on the roof of the Party Headquarters to be met by the same generals, Securitate officers and Communist Party functionaries who had waved goodbye to the presidential couple on their last fateful journey. They all wore the same hats, yet they were now very different. 'Viva the revolution! Romania libera!' they chorused, waving their hats, much as they had done just hours earlier when they chanted 'Ni-co-lae Cea-oooo-şes-cooo . . . Romaneeeeaaah!'

The change in their demeanour was nothing short of miraculous. They had shed their Party badges, unclenched their fists and went about hugging each other in an ecstasy of self-congratulation. Gone was every trace of banners and bunting, along with portraits of the beloved leader. A life-time's solemn, sincere, dogged attachment to the Party had vanished overnight.

So complete was the transformation that Jimfish's head began to spin like a giddy top. The men who led this revolution were surely the same officials who willingly murdered, harried, spied on and lied to the very people in the square all through the long rule of the late dictator. Who had flinched in horror when the crowds dared to boo the Genius of the Carpathians and who fled for the roof when the crowds, revved up on the rocket fuel of lumpen-proletarian rage, invaded Party Headquarters.

When Jimfish asked them what they felt about Nicolae and Elena's show trial they looked at him as if he were quite mad. When he admitted that he had been saddened by the firing squad in Târgovişte, they laughed outright. Was he, they demanded, a counter-revolutionary?

'We fought for freedom and defeated the tyrant. Finishing him off was the best Christmas present in the world. We have given the people what they wanted: the dictator is dead. Anyone who can't see that is an enemy of the revolution.'

With that they beat Jimfish savagely about the head and might have killed him had he not run into the very lift that had once saved Nicolae from the angry mob. The lift descended to the ground floor and Jimfish escaped into the giant square in front of Party Headquarters, where a vast crowd was still camped in their threadbare coats, cold and hungry, watching on a large screen scenes from the execution of Nicolae and Elena, replayed day and night, as if this were all the food they needed, and the images of the bloody end of these two monsters was also the end of tyranny and terror. While to Jimfish – ashamed though he was of his negative thoughts – it seemed as if the way the Ceauşescus had died, rather than killing off the past, had given the old demons a new lease of life, free to haunt the country for years to come.

As he turned away from the ghastly images, a tall, elegant black man in a dove-grey tunic, wearing on his head a leopard-skin toque, offered Jimfish his silk handkerchief.

'Wipe the blood from your eyes, my friend.'

The stranger wore heavy black spectacles and he carried a wooden sceptre, surmounted by a leopard.

'How sad to find these crowds rejoicing at the murder of their Great Leader. We would never allow this in Africa.'

For the first time since the loss of Lunamiel, the murder of Jagdish and the shooting of Soviet Malala, Jimfish felt happiness rising inside him like the sun and he grasped the other's hand. 'My compatriot! I'm from the Mother Continent, too. My name is Jimfish of Port Pallid, a tiny town on the eastern coast of South Africa.'

The other lifted his sceptre in salute. 'And I am Marshal Mobutu Sese Seko Nkuku Ngbendu wa Za Banga – which is to say, "The All-powerful, Earthy, Fiery Warrior Who, through His Endurance and Inflexible Will to Win, Moves from Conquest to Conquest, Trailing Fire in His Wake". I am the embodiment of Zaire, a country twenty per cent bigger than Mexico and very, very rich in diamonds and minerals. You may call me the Great Leopard.'

Jimfish complimented the gentleman on the size and wealth of his homeland.

'Far more than a simple homeland,' said the other. 'Zaire is my personal invention. The very appellation, along with what my citizens are allowed to wear or name themselves, as well as how my nation's riches are spent, are all extensions of my dreams. A country that began as a land of slaves and sadness, which greedy European imperialists called the Belgian Congo, is now, thanks to my vision, the glorious, authentic Republic of Zaire. People know me as its Great Marshal, Grand Chief and Messiah.'

'And you were a friend of the late Nicolae and Elena Ceauşescu?' Jimfish guessed.

The gentleman held up two fingers tightly pressed together. 'We were as close as this. Brothers under the skin. Imagine how I felt when, on Christmas Day, lying in bed in my palace, I tuned into satellite television to find myself witnessing the Genius of the Carpathians being done to death by barbarians. I ordered my jet to be made ready and flew post-haste here to Bucharest, hoping at least to arrange for my old friend a state funeral in Zaire. Too late, alas. Why do those who killed the great Ceauşescu not see they had the leader they deserved? A reflection of themselves?'

Jimfish reported what he had been told. 'They called him a cruel tyrant.'

'Cruelty in a leader is often plain common sense. In my country, for example, some say I don't bother to feed my prisoners. But why should I, when I can't even feed my own peasants? However, cruelty needs to be judiciously employed . . . I once had the pleasure of hanging four of my ministers in a popular public ceremony, attended by fifty thousand enthusiastic citizens. It was on the feast of Pentecost, as it happens. Punishment is all the more impressive – I speak as a fervent Catholic – when combined with piety. Murder, *tout seul*, is a clumsy tool. Better to pay off your rivals or have them done away with discreetly or buy them back into government on your own terms. Genial corruption is the key. Steal if you like, I counsel my ministers, soldiers and gendarmes – but not too much – and not all at once. That way you win more.'

'What I can't fathom about those who killed the Genius of the Carpathians and his wife,' said Jimfish, 'is their reasoning. They were socialists yesterday, call themselves democrats now and yet they beat those who disagree.'

The gentleman in the leopard-skin toque shook his head sadly. 'We will never understand the reasoning of Europeans, if they possess anything of the sort worth bothering with. Western ways have no place in Africa and that's why I have abolished Christian names. They're nothing but sentimental western affectations, so I have banned them. And business suits may no longer be worn. They're symbols of the old imperialism. Not fitting for the tiger-daughters and lion-sons of the New Africa, who deserve real leaders. In our tradition we have room only for one chief, one Big Man.'

'Surely some opposition is good in a democracy?' Jimfish asked.

'In our authentic Zairean system, democracy is the foundation on which the leader bases his divine right to rule. When opposition is needed, I provide it by calling an election and standing against the President. That way voters may choose freely between me and myself, but there can be only one winner.'

Jimfish was a little confused by this. 'I take it, then, you don't like change?'

The tall man smiled and waved his wooden sceptre. 'I am warming to it all the time. But it must be carefully managed. Many of the greatest African leaders have been in power for decades, thanks to their understanding of the proper use of elections. When I consider what I call the Ceauşescu conundrum, I think I see where he went wrong. Freedom is better than stagnation and repression, so long as it's regulated. I begin to think encouraging democracy and allowing several parties to compaign might be useful. Why should I be held to account for everything? Let them also share the blame.'

Jimfish returned the borrowed and now bloody silk handkerchief to his new friend.

'The Romanians could profit from your advice. As far as I can see, and I may be wrong, those running their revolution look like the same people who ran the old regime.'

The gentleman from Zaire nodded. 'No doubt. And mark my words, soon they will be claiming the high moral ground and lecturing African leaders about their appalling habits. This is the way of Europeans. They enslave Africa, pillage the continent and then preach sermons to their former slaves. I prefer their lash to their lectures. Enough of savage Europe. You need to get home again and I can help. Come with me.'

With that the elegant stranger in the leopard-skin toque took a handful of dollars from his Vuitton bag, hailed a taxi and they rode out to the airport. There on the tarmac was a most beautiful needle-nosed jet, which, his friend from Zaire explained, he rented from the French. Jimfish was greatly impressed. What a people these French must be! The cloud of radioactive dust from Chernobyl had stopped at their border and then gone around the sides of the country. And supersonic jets were loans they lavished on African heads of state.

'Since we are compatriots,' said Sese Seko, 'let us dispense with titles for a while. At least in private. You are called Jimfish . . . Well, when I was a boy at the Christian Brothers College, in what was then Elizabethville, my name was Joseph-Désiré, but the other boys called me Jeff.'

It was agreed they would maintain this friendly informality, at least until they returned home, when Jimfish would have a variety of choices as to the name he preferred for his new friend: Messiah, Lion King, Redeemer, Guide or Great Helmsman. And so it was that, in the spirit of school friends, Jimfish and Jeff boarded the waiting Concorde and flew off to Africa.

CHAPTER 12

Zaire/Gbadolite, 1989–90

The needle-nosed jet taxied along the runway in trop-
ical sunshine and Jimfish was glad to be home, even if this
Africa of red dust and dark green bush was one he did not
know. On the flight from Bucharest he had been pampered
with caviar and Laurent-Perrier champagne, which, along
with Coca-Cola, was the favourite beverage of the inven-
tor of Zaire, whose destiny was an extension of his dreams,
and who now gently reminded Jimfish that – as he was
back in his country and must take on again the duties of
his office – there would be no more schoolboy names.

'Which of my many titles would you feel happiest to
use? You may choose any one of them. Feel free, my fellow
African friend.'

'"Great Leopard" seems the best suited, I think.
Especially because of your signature hat,' Jimfish told him.

His companion was delighted, because it showed how
well Jimfish understood his very special relationship with
the Mother Continent – something his compatriots too
often failed to grasp.

'A very wise choice. I have my toques specially made for me in Paris, using only the fur of leopards I myself have shot. As principal protector of the royal beasts of Africa I can assure you that the leopard selected to become my headgear counts itself lucky to crown an intellect of such distinction.'

Jimfish was impressed by the other's unassailable certainty, as well as his remarkable ability to adapt to all circumstances, even if this left him a trifle uneasy. It was a flexibility he had seen in the men who executed Nicolae and Elena Ceauşescu on Christmas Day, and who turned overnight from cowering flunkeys into incendiary revolutionaries. How he wished he might achieve a smidgeon of their adaptability or feel even a tenth of their revolutionary rage.

His found his deficiencies in both these qualities very distressing. Surely he had seen enough cruelty and heartbreak in the time since fleeing Port Pallid, moments before Sergeant Arlow could shoot him? He had been present at the massacres in Matabeleland led by General Jesus; endured the loss of his lovely Lunamiel, cruelly blown to bits as she said her prayers; watched helplessly as Ivan the Russian murdered the good Jagdish at Chernobyl; and he had looked on helplessly as his mentor Soviet Malala was executed by a drunken firing squad in the doomed city of Pripyat.

But now he was home once again. It was Boxing Day, the New Year and a new decade of the Nineties lay ahead, and Jimfish made it his New Year's resolution to try harder than ever to burn with the fury that fired the lumpenproletariat to a happy landing on the right side of history.

In a giant, open-topped limousine, flanked by motorcycle outriders and Horse Guards – splendid in uniforms based on those worn by Napoleon's cavalry – the Great Leopard and his friend progressed from the spanking-new airport, where the runways had been specially lengthened to allow the Concorde to land, into a town called Gbadolite. Chanting crowds lined the route and Marshal Mobutu translated the praise song they repeated: 'One party, one country, one father – Mobutu!' He waved his wooden sceptre to acknowledge the cheers.

Almost everyone in the town was related to Seso Seko Mobutu, he told Jimfish proudly, and they all adored him.

'I am bound to my people by pure love. But what good is love if it doesn't take very concrete forms? It is as simple as that, you will find.'

Simple was not at all what Jimfish found.

What had been a tiny village was now a thriving city of thousands. His friend pointed out the German-run hospital, the new sawmill, the factories, the impressive dam to supply hydroelectric power, the experimental breeding farm stocked with thoroughbred English cows and Swiss goats, the Coca-Cola plant, and, last but not least, the Central Bank of Zaire, where printing presses worked day and night to produce bushels of banknotes adorned with the image of the leader in his leopard-skin hat.

Gbadolite was his home town, and 'Home for a king,' the marshal explained, 'is where your palace stands.'

Ahead loomed a colossal palace ringed by a high fence.

Sentries saluted as the limousine swept through the gates of gold and drew up at the main door, which was bracketed by enormous pink marble columns and guarded by four life-size white marble lions. In the palace gardens stood towering sculptures of elephants, lions and buffaloes, while peacocks wandered at will among pools, fountains and waterfalls.

Jimfish was lost in admiration. 'It is a palace in the forest!'

Marshal Mobutu nodded. 'It's known as Versailles in the Jungle. I have a second one nearby, a pagoda, built for me by the Chinese. And somewhere' – he made a vague gesture towards the thick green bush that surrounded the estate – 'is a third. But I lose track of them. After all, I own a castle in Spain, a palace in Switzerland, capacious residences in Paris, the Riviera, Belgium, Italy, the Ivory Coast, Senegal, South Africa and Portugal. Not to mention a string of palaces that adorn Zaire like a lovely necklace, stretching from Kinshasa to Lubumbashi. To me a palace is just one more place to hang my hat.'

Seeing his friend's incomprehension at this prodigious display, the Great Leopard said soothingly: 'I don't do this for myself, but because I know my people. I understand how much they admire glamour. They are too poor to afford anything themselves. So someone must take up the challenge on their behalf. I sacrifice myself in the name of peace. We have over two hundred ethnic groups in Zaire and I am the magic that melds them together.'

In what was clearly a customary ceremony of welcome, a butler led in a young leopard on a silver chain and pre-

71

sented it to the Great Leopard, who in turn introduced his pet to Jimfish.

'This is Simba, my friend and brother.'

The leopard looked at Jimfish and he looked at the leopard. It seemed a shame to keep a big cat on a chain, but he was too polite to say so.

'Come, let's go to my office,' the marshal proposed.

Up the spiral Italian staircase he led Jimfish, beneath great crystal chandeliers flowering from tall ceilings, followed by butlers, valets, pages, chefs, housemaids and praise singers, while from speakers hidden in the walls came the plaintive chant of Gregorian monks.

The presidential office seemed about the size of a tennis court and, after opening the safe and stuffing his favourite Vuitton bag with hundred-dollar bills, they moved into the presidential bedroom. It was dominated by an immense bed of sculpted marble in the shape of a pink cross. Jimfish was invited to seat himself beside the Great Leopard, and then, at the touch of a button, like an ascending elevator, the great bed climbed smoothly until it was level with the windows. Gathered in the gardens below was a large, excited crowd.

'My relatives,' the President explained, throwing fistfuls of dollar bills from the window, beaming to see his devoted family fighting for their share as the greenbacks rained down. 'This ceremony encourages loyalty and love and competition. My advice over the years, to poor Nicolae, was to keep your friends close and your enemies closer still. I wish he had listened to me.'

Once the distribution of dollars was over, palace tailors

came and took Jimfish's measurements, and returned a few hours later with a set of splendid clothes. The Great Leopard having forbidden all western costume in his country, the craftsmen had sewn for Jimfish a tunic of gun-metal grey that echoed the President's. It had a pert collar, worn with an olive-green silk cravat. He was also presented with a ceremonial pistol in a holster of python skin to be worn on formal occasions. In each pocket of his tunic he found neat stacks of hundred-dollar bills, placed there by his ever-thoughtful friend the Great Leopard, who, when Jimfish tried to thank him, brushed aside his gratitude.

'You are my African brother,' he said. 'It is I who must thank you for helping me to find another recipient for a very small part of my fortune.'

There was to be a great banquet that evening with more pink champagne, truffles, foie gras, shrimp, quail and caviar to celebrate the safe return of the Redeemer to his people. But Jimfish had begun to feel the strain of his travels and pleaded to be allowed an early night, to which his host graciously assented.

And so it was that Jimfish found himself alone in a bedroom, itself as large as the old trawler captain's house in Port Pallid. Before sleeping, he switched on the giant TV and watched the evening news bulletin. It opened with a portrait of Mobuto Sese Seko, Beloved Leader, Solitary Sun, Incomparable Helmsman, shown descending from heaven, garlanded with golden rays, while unseen choirs hymned his incomparable genius. There followed film of their arrival at the airport of Gbadolite and scenes of his relatives massing in the palace gardens to receive the rain

73

of dollars. The nightly newscast closed with the Blessed Redeemer of Zaire ascending to heaven to the accompaniment of harps and trumpets.

Unable to keep his eyes open a moment longer, Jimfish fell fast asleep wearing his splendid new suit of clothes, with his ceremonial pistol in its holster of python skin. So dead to the world was he that, when he felt someone shaking him gently, he was sure he was dreaming.

He opened his eyes to find a black lady swathed in a silver veil, who bent over him and whispered: 'Follow me and you will be very, very happy.'

When he asked what this happiness might be, she touched her finger to his lips and whispered, 'Trust me, Jimfish.'

Chapter 13

Down a long, dimly lit passage and into another part
of the palace, the veiled woman led Jimfish, seemingly
knowing her way by instinct. She showed him into a room
furnished with a fine red sofa and enormous tapestries,
woven with hunting scenes of kings and knights pursuing
wild boar. Here she told Jimfish to wait. He sat on the red
sofa and pondered the tapestry. The hunters on their giant
horses, their lances buried in the bleeding bellies of the
snarling boars, and in the corner of the scene he saw the
emblem of the President himself, a leopard on a chain,
lunging at the prey.

Yet despite the carnage in the tapestries, the atmosphere
seemed to Jimfish softer and less brazenly opulent than he
had found it in the rest of the palace.

After a little while, the door opened and in came his
guide, leading by the hand a woman, who held before her
face a carnival mask. Jimfish jumped to his feet when she
entered. There was something about her that made him
sink back again on the sofa, his heart hammering his

ribcage. At a sign from her attendant, the lady lowered her mask and there she was: his beloved Lunamiel, as lustrous and luscious as the day he had seen her last in faraway Port Pallid, when, lying on the red picnic rug in her father's orchard, he and she had become as entangled as the tendrils of the strangler fig.

It was all too much for poor Jimfish, still dizzy and exhausted by the events of the past days, and he fainted. When he came to, he was stretched full length on the sofa, his head in Lunamiel's lap, struggling to make sense of it all, while she dabbed his lips and temples with a handkerchief dipped in cooling cologne.

'But they told me you were dead,' Jimfish whispered. 'That you were in church one Sunday when a bomb blew you to bits.'

'But for the grace of God I would have been blown to bits,' Lunamiel said. 'Such outrages were common in our country in the mad mid-1980s when everyone was at war. Whites were shooting blacks, blacks were bombing whites and each side was ready to destroy the other. But as it happened, I wasn't in church that day – thanks to a miracle. My brother, Deon – who you will remember vowed to shoot you if ever he found you – had the luck to meet a rich Zairean businessman who promised him the deal of a lifetime if he would travel to the Congo to meet the Great Leopard, at the time dealing secretly with our government. Deon was offered exclusive mineral rights – cobalt, copper, gold, diamonds or all of them – if he provided strategic advice to the leader of Zaire, who had a problem very common across Africa. The President was immensely rich and his people were starving. The question that plagued Sese Seko Mobutu and dozens of leaders like him was easy to state but hard to solve: how does a Big Man deal with the needs of poor people and still keep everything he has?'

'Certainly, that is a hard question,' Jimfish agreed. 'And I'd say impossible to solve. You can have either one or the other.'

Lunamiel agreed. 'But that was the test: if my brother came up with the answer he'd be a millionaire.'

Jimfish was pleased: perhaps Deon Arlow had some qualities he'd not heard of back in Port Pallid. 'And your brother agreed to help?'

'He did. But it took a considerable struggle with his conscience. He is a real white South African who had been taught, ever since he was very, very small, to distrust and dismiss other black Africans. But when it came to business, Deon was a great adapter and he could turn his coat quicker than anyone I ever knew. Whenever Deon crossed the South African on business he behaved in a manner so refined you might call it almost human. Deon knew his duty was to do business in Zaire, though of course he said nothing to our father, wishing to spare his feelings. And that is why, when the bomb exploded beneath the altar of my church in Port Pallid on that Sunday morning, ripping to shreds any number of worshippers, my brother and I were sipping champagne in first-class seats, high above the Victoria Falls, on a flight to Kinshasa.'

'It's a miracle!' said Jimfish.

'Someone has to pay for other people's miracles,' said

Lunamiel. 'Sadly, my father, believing I was indeed dead, set off to punish those he suspected of planting the bomb, shooting many of them, just as he would have shot you, my dear Jimfish, had you not fled the garden that day we sat together. As it happened, the men he killed were not the perpetrators of the attack. Agents of our own government had planted the bomb in church with what they regarded as the laudable intention of laying the blame at the door of black terrorists.'

'How sad and ironic,' said Jimfish.

'Exactly so,' said Lunamiel. 'As you will see when I tell you that the very next Sunday, when my father and mother went to church to pray for me, they were themselves blown to bits by a bomb, placed beneath the altar, by the remaining members of the black liberation movement whom my father had not managed to shoot.'

'How terrible!' Jimfish was horrified at the painful symmetry of these violent acts.

'And sad and ironic,' Lunamiel agreed with a wan smile. 'Both sides in our homegrown war now felt it was quits, at least for a while. But how did you come to be here, my dear Jimfish? I want to know everything that has happened since you fled Port Pallid for Zimbabwe and the outside world.'

So Jimfish hugged her tightly and told her of his travels in Matabeleland, his work as a bio-robot on the roof of Reactor Number 4 at Chernobyl, of the treacherous murder of the good Jagdish and the death of Soviet Malala, his unforgettable teacher. And, hearing his adventures, Lunamiel was moved to tears more than once.

'Do you think it's the fate of South Africans to end badly?' he asked Lunamiel.

She sighed. 'Since arriving in this country I've heard it said over and over that the only good South African is a dead South African. And when I tell you what has happened to me, you may ask yourself whether death is not a desirable option.'

And with Jimfish hanging on her every word, side by side on the red sofa, she told him her story.

CHAPTER 14

'My brother Deon is not only flexible in his principles and pragmatic in his business practices, he is positively elastic in family matters. We had not been in Zaire more than a few days when he enlightened me as to my role in his business.

'"You are not merely my dear sister," he explained. "You are going to play a vital role in the deal I've signed with a Big Man in the court of the Great Leopard. No less a personage than his Minister of Mines."

'When I asked, very gently, why I had not been consulted before he signed the deal, Deon explained my great good fortune to me.

'"Not many people get the chance to change the world. And the world I'm talking about is the one that condemns white South Africans as incorrigible racists who despise black people. You will prove them wrong, my dear sister, by showing how eager we are to engage constructively with our African compatriots. In doing so, you will also improve our own balance of payments."'

Lunamiels's eyes flashed, as they did when she was angry.

'I must admit I was rather impatient and demanded to know how a girl from Port Pallid would improve anyone's balance of payments.

'"Perfectly simple," said Deon. "The Congo of the Great Leopard has lots of cobalt, copper, cadmium, petroleum, diamonds, gold, bauxite and tin, just to mention some of its riches. For a percentage, I've arranged for you to engage with the Minister of Mines most constructively, day and night, and the idea excites him hugely."

'My brother had no sooner introduced me to the Minister of Mines than I understood the nature of this excitement, because he flung me down on a nearby bed, saying that he had always wanted a white South African woman. All this I suffered in the cause of constructive engagement and to show my white compatriots in a better light.'

Jimfish again hugged her close, feeling within him the very first stirrings of anger.

'My darling Lunamiel, a prisoner of this man's lust! How long has this been going on?'

But she reassured him sweetly. 'Not long at all. Luckily for me, a few days later, the Minister of Mines died suddenly during a diamond dealers' conference held here in the palace at Gbadolite.'

'He had some sort of accident?' asked Jimfish.

Lunamiel sighed at the memory. 'He was shot to death with poisoned arrows by a squadron of pygmies, which the Zairean army keeps for the purpose. But my relief did not last long. I soon discovered that I had been designated the bedfellow of the Minister of Education, who had arranged for his colleague's accident in a very Zairean cabinet reshuffle.'

'A godsend!' Jimfish clapped his hands in relief. 'Because education elevates the mind, as my dear teacher Soviet Malala used to say.'

Lunamiel shook her head. 'In Zaire, the Minister of Education is there to make sure nothing of the sort ever happens and he was constantly crushing student riots and closing the national university.'

'How appalling!' cried Jimfish.

'Not entirely,' Lunamiel explained gently. 'This work took up a good deal of his day, as well as a considerable proportion of his nights, and I was spared his constant demands. But I had caught the eye of another high official, the secret American Advisor to the President. The Great Leopard has enjoyed American backing ever since he came to power, after eliminating Patrice Lumumba, the first elected leader of the Congo. Successive US presidents call him their very special African friend and vital ally against their enemies abroad, and give him bushels of money, as well as tons of guns.'

Jimfish still felt rather relieved. 'If the Americans are so fond of the Great Leopard, then you must have found a powerful protector in the secret agent.'

Lunamiel sighed. 'If only that were so. Instead, I was now the object of desire of the Minister of Education as well as the American and they could never agree on a timetable. My minister insisted that I was his sole property, under the terms of the contract made by my brother with the late Minister of Mines. But my American, who came from the Deep South, swore that the Bible forbids a white girl to cohabit with a black man and I owed it to God to sleep only with a white Christian.

'Each rival vied with the other by mounting manly displays of strength and daring, hoping to impress me. My minister would take me to Lubumbashi University and make me watch as he dealt with rebellious students, whom he might shoot or blind or bury in pits, depending on his mood. Only to have my American admirer riposte with a display of the latest US chemical defoliants, to prove how easily he could devastate the forest for miles around. Or he'd call up a bombing raid on a village in the jungle. My minister would then up the ante by arranging a front-row seat for me at the public hanging of several high officials; an event preceded by marching bands and much revelry, and concluded, while the bodies were being taken down from the gallows, with caviar and pink champagne, as is the custom in the court of the Great Leopard. My American condemned this behaviour as cruel and barbaric, and countered by offering to take me home to his country, marry me in his evangelical church and give me a ringside seat at all executions by electric chair in his home state, which, apparently, boasted the world record.

'Eventually, the two rivals agreed on a roster: they would enjoy me alternately, on a timeshare basis. So it was that I became my minister's bedmate and nocturnal amusement over the weekends, from Friday to Sunday, when he rested from eradicating students and accompanied the Great

Leopard to Sunday Mass, a ritual he never missed. But from Monday to Thursday it was agreed I would belong to my American.

'But soon enough the rivals fell out. My minister insisted I remain his bedfellow right through Sunday night until Monday morning, whereas my God-fearing American, who punctiliously observed the Sabbath day of rest, demanded that I come to his bed on the stroke of Sunday midnight, as soon as the constraints of the Sabbath fell away. This argument has gone on for months and I have had the pleasure of escaping both rivals, while they quarrel over which of them has more favoured rights to my person.

'Then, tonight, I saw on the television the arrival of the Great Leopard in his French needle-nosed supersonic jet, and who should step out of the aircraft but my own dear, darling Jimfish, with his tawny hair and his strange complexion, not white nor brown nor black but golden, whom I had last seen in the orchard, when we lay together on the red rug and my father beat you and would have shot you dead had he not tripped over his own feet. And so I sent my attendant to bring you to my apartments.'

'And I am here and we are together again!' Jimfish put his arms around his beloved Lunamiel.

The kindly attendant, who had been Jimfish's guide, slipped away, leaving the lovers to their happiness. Lunamiel drew Jimfish down beside her on the red sofa, their breathing quickened, their clothing loosened and they were soon as entangled as ever they had been in Sergeant Arlow's orchard, when into the room there strode the

Minister of Education, rampant with desire, for it was already late on Sunday night and he was keen to assert his right to Lunamiel's delectable body before midnight struck and his timeshare ran out.

CHAPTER 15

'You two-faced, scheming, white South African bitch!' yelled the Minister of Education. 'Isn't it enough that you screw that damn American five nights a week? Must I also share you with this human shrimp, this pale pastiche of a man?'

And he hurled himself at Jimfish, beating him savagely, and would have killed him, as was his way when dealing with students who troubled him. Lunamiel let out a terrific wail, but Jimfish acted with a decisiveness that astonished them both: he pulled out the pearl-handled pistol from its python-skin holster – a gift of the Great Leopard – and calmly shot the minister, who fell dead on the sofa, bleeding everywhere.

Jimfish apologized for the mess, but Lunamiel, ever practical, told him not to give it a second thought. The sofa was red, so was the minister's blood, and the stains would hardly be noticed.

'But what does worry me a bit is that the President's gendarmes will arrive and find a close ally of the Great

Leopard dead in my apartment. Then we're done for.'

Jimfish longed to know what Soviet Malala might have advised. When the Minister of Education had begun beating him, Jimfish thought he felt again, as he had done when Lunamiel was relating how she had been contracted to the lecherous Minister of Mines, a rising warmth, which he prayed might be a sign of the rage that is the rocket fuel of the lumpenproletariat. But his old teacher lay dead in faraway Ukraine, so he asked the kindly attendant, who had brought him to Lunamiel's apartment, if she had an idea what they should do now?

Just as she agreed to share her ideas with them, the clock struck midnight and into the room burst the American advisor, as rampant with desire for the luscious body of Lunamiel as had been his late rival, the Minister of Education. This American, hardened though he was by demonstrations of the damage defoliants do to fertile soils or cluster bombs to enemy farmers in the fields, was shocked to see the co-proprietor of his timeshare agreement to Lunamiel's body stretched lifeless on the red sofa.

Jimfish knew he had to act fast. The American was capable of pulling out a machine gun or calling in a bombing raid. Whispering to himself, 'in for a penny, in for a pound,' he shot the raging American between the eyes and saw him topple on to the sofa, where his blood mingled with that of his rival.

Jimfish felt strangely relaxed, and he asked himself once again – as he had done when he saw the fawning henchmen of Nicolae Ceauşescu transformed into liberators of their country by the adroit application of a firing squad – whether it was not perhaps adaptability rather than anger, pragmatism and not principles, firepower and not fury that was the real rocket fuel of the lumpenproletariat? Or, for that matter, of just about anyone in possession of overwhelming force who proved fastest on the draw? In other words: was it not the case of murder first – and morality later?

Lunamiel was frozen between terror and admiration. 'I'd never have believed you could be so wild and angry. You've just shot two men dead without thinking twice.'

Jimfish enjoyed a tremor of self-esteem, though he replied very modestly. 'When you've worked as a bio-robot on the roof of a crippled nuclear reactor leaking radiation, and seen your friend and mentor executed by a drunken Ukrainian firing squad, you begin to get a little worked up. At least, I hope so.'

Lunamiel's kindly attendant now gave her views on their situation. 'We will all be punished when the gendarmerie arrive. That is their way. We must get out of this appalling country, where the lives of women are hell.'

'What are you saying?' Jimfish asked. 'The Great Leopard is the kindest of men. He has created, out of the old Belgian Congo, a free country where the shackles of European slavery have been thrown off, the very names of the old colonialists are forbidden and no one dares to wear a business suit. When he finds out how Lunamiel was bought and sold as the sex slave of a ruthless American agent, as well as a homicidal Minister of Education, not only will he open his heart to her, but also his Vuitton suitcase and shower her with wealth, as I have seen him do to his extended family.'

'You are badly mistaken,' said the dark lady. 'Appealing to the Great Leopard will make things very much worse. When you hear my tale you will understand why. Our leader is an obsessive sexual maniac, a constant deflowerer of virgins, a compulsive adulterer and a wife-stealer.'

'Are we are talking of the same man?' Jimfish was flabbergasted. 'Do you mean the President of Zaire, whose authentic tribal name of Mobutu Sese Seko Nkuku Ngbendu wa Za Banga actually means "The All-powerful, Earthy, Fiery Warrior Who, through His Endurance and Inflexible Will to Win, Moves from Conquest to Conquest, Trailing Fire in His Wake"?'

'The very same,' said his informant. 'But those of us who speak his language translate his name in quite another way. We call him: "The Cockerel Who Screws All the Chicks in the Henhouse". And I should know. I was once an innocent young girl from faraway Liberia, where my family betrothed me to an important Congolese entrepreneur, who promised them gold and diamonds and pink champagne. As it happened, this gentleman was the very same Minister of Mines you have heard so much about. Very soon after I arrived here, my husband deserted me and I was thrown on to the street. Marshal Mobutu decrees that divorce, desertion or cruelty are what women are destined for and he has made it an offence to protest. He encourages husbands to desert their wives on a whim, neglect their children and marry as often as they like. Our President also believes he has droit de seigneur, so he sleeps in turn with the wives of all his cabinet ministers and I happen to know your cherished Lunamiel is next on his list.'

'Imagine that! Your late husband was the same man to whom my brother Deon offered me on long lease!' Lunamiel shook her head in disbelief. 'Luckily, he was shot to death by the squadron of pygmies kept by the Great Leopard for the purpose.'

'It was a blessing for you, perhaps, but my luck ran out long ago,' said the dark lady, dabbing away a tear with her silver veil. 'After I was abandoned by my husband, I was targeted by bands of mutinous soldiers who had gone for months unpaid and took out their anger on women like me. I was made the plaything of pimps and used as bait by brothel-keepers. From the lovely young girl I had been when I came to the Congo, I crumbled into a wreck; my looks went, then my pride and my spirit. In the end I had no choice but to work as a servant, and when I saw this young white South African girl given as the other half of a timeshare contract to the late Minister of Education, I decided to save her from the horrors I had faced. After all, she was South African and clearly knew nothing at all about Africa. But then again, white South Africans, being the last of the employing classes, she would know how to treat domestic help with kindness. But her background and yours will be fatal when the marshal's cruel gendamerie find us.' The dark lady indicated the two bodies bleeding on the red sofa. 'To have shot dead a minister in the cabinet of Marshal Mobutu is never a problem; he will be replaced in hours. But to have gunned down an American agent, when it is the Americans who have faithfully bankrolled the Great Leopard throughout his long reign as the King of the Congo, is asking for trouble. Let's go – and quickly!'

'But where can we go – and how?' asked Lunamiel.

'Come with me,' said the dark lady. 'In the garages of the Great Leopard is a fleet of limousines, keys in the ignition, the petrol tanks full. Each is ready to roll because no one knows which the President may choose or when he may have to leave in a hurry.'

CHAPTER 16

After inspecting the fleet of limousines in the presidential garage, they chose – on the advice of Lunamiel's knowledgeable servant – a Mercedes-Benz S600 Pullman. It was a vast black vehicle with creamy leather seats, walnut dashboard and a bar stocked with pink champagne. Its passenger windows were hung with heavy curtains that gave it the look of a catafalque on wheels.

The dark lady knew all about these splendid machines and their reputation for reliability amongst self-respecting leaders, who risked their lives to bring peace and stability to their often ungrateful peoples.

'Nicolae Ceauşescu it was who told Marshal Mobutu that if he wished to travel in a style commensurate with his majesty, then only the Mercedes Pullman would do. It is the limo of choice among serious big men around the planet, from Marshal Tito and Mao Zedong, to the Shah of Persia. Colonel Gaddafi, Guide and Leader of Libya, hands them out as gifts, and my own President Samuel Doe, liberator of Liberia, owns half a dozen. I've even heard that Erich Honecker of East Germany liked to hunt deer by the strength of its headlights.'

Jimfish was dumbfounded by the sheer immensity of the limousine. 'If we're using it to escape, why not take something a bit less conspicuous?'

'Size isn't everything,' the lady agreed. 'But this Mercedes is also bullet-proof and that's very important indeed.'

She turned out to be even wiser than Jimfish had imagined. On their journey through Zaire they were fired upon several times by gangs of soldiers who roamed the countryside, demanding bribes, robbing, raping and pillaging, but their armour-plated automobile shrugged off bullets as a buffalo does flies.

As they rolled along the potholed roads, in between attacks and ambushes, Lunamiel's attendant told them her story.

'You wouldn't think so to look at me, but I am a princess of the Krahn tribe. Our people were local and truly at home in a part of Africa which later came to be called Liberia, when American settlers arrived, unasked, and took over. These new arrivals never amounted to more than a fraction of the original people of Liberia, but they ran our country as a one-party state. They saw to it that Americans and *only* Americans ruled the roost, and treated us as dunces or domestic servants.'

Jimfish remembered how things were done in Port Pallid, where Sergeant Arlow's wife Gloriosa – so unfortunately blown to smithereens as she and her husband attended Sunday service – had kept not just a retinue of retainers for everything from cooking to the act of conception, but had even assigned separate servants to each hand when her fingernails needed care. Did he at last feel stirring within him the elements of what he hoped might be the heat that ignites to form the rage that is the rocket fuel of the lumpenproletariat? Certainly a painful longing for home took hold of him.

'I know exactly what you mean! We had the very same in my country. In our case it was whites who ruled the roost, though they amounted to a fraction of the population. They were arrogant, stupid, lazy latecomers to Africa, colonialists, imperialists and slave-drivers, who saw themselves as God's privileged people.'

'It was something like that,' said the dark lady. 'Except that our American invaders were black and not white. They were freed slaves or their descendants, whose relatives had been shipped from Africa to work the cotton fields of the southern states and now came back to the Mother Continent to lord it over real Africans. When we rebelled they punished us and ordered us to enjoy the liberty they had brought to (their name, not ours) "Liberia".'

'Well, I suppose,' said the kindly Lunamiel, 'that by freeing their slaves and transporting them back home the Americans thought they were being kind.'

'I dare say,' their attendant nodded. 'But in my experience Americans are never more dangerous than when doing good. Especially when they go to war in order to save those less fortunate than themselves. Naturally, we real Africans didn't like their attitude. My tribe, the Krahn, had never accepted slavery. When others around us fell to the slavers, the Krahn would kill themselves rather than be sold and shipped to the USA. It was my Krahn people who produced a saviour who threw off decades of Americo-Liberian hegemony. Our very own Master Sergeant Samuel Doe bravely attacked the presidential palace one night some ten years ago and killed President William Tolbert, who led a regime full of those we called "settler-class people", while they called us "country people". Some say that, perhaps, Master Sergeant Doe should not have gone on to murder President Tolbert's ministers – that shooting thirteen of them, soon after the coup, was taking things a bit far. But you must understand we were still feeling our way.'

Jimfish, who had seen much blood flow since leaving Port Pallid, was somewhat sensitive to the sight of executions, and when he heard how Tolbert's deposed ministers were dragged to a beach in Monrovia, bound to steel poles and shot by jeering soldiers, he could not help shaking his head. Even Nicolae and Elena Ceauşescu had been given a show trial before being executed.

'Was there no better way?' Jimfish asked.

The dark lady regretted there was not. 'Surely it was kinder to shoot these criminals all at once, rather than drag things out by executing them over several days? It was vital to show everyone that in the new Liberia no one was favoured because of rank or office, and that we indigenous people were in charge at last. That's why those shot on the beach included the Speaker of the House, a one-time Budget Director, a former Chief Justice and quite a few members of the late President's family.'

'And yet there was no trial?' Jimfish asked.

'No time for that,' said the lady. 'Such was the people's rage against the tyrannical ex-President Tolbert.'

On hearing the word 'rage' Jimfish felt a little easier – for, after all, wasn't it anger that grew in heat till it vaporized into white-hot rage that was the rocket fuel of the lumpenproletariat? And if, in his heart of hearts, he found unsettling the portrait this lady painted of the trembling ministers on the beach, beaten, tormented and made to wait in line due to a shortage of steel poles, until they were cut to pieces with long bursts of automatic rifle fire by drunken soldiers, he told himself that this was probably what it took if you wanted to land on the right side of history.

Realizing he was confused, Lunamiel's attendant added kindly: 'There was no trial of these criminals. But nothing was hidden or underhand. Because he knew the world was watching, and in the interests of transparency, Master Sergeant Doe and his Redemption Council invited the press to the executions on the beach and encouraged them to film the proceedings for posterity.'

The kindly Lunamiel wept at the story, overcome by homesickness for her house, garden and orchard in Port Pallid, remembering her mother and father, blown to pieces while at their Sunday prayers. But she soon cheered up when Jimfish hugged her tenderly and promised to take her home to South Africa just as soon as he could.

Their giant limousine carried them safely from Gbadolite to Kinshasa and on to the port of Boma on the north bank of Congo river, some miles upstream from the sea, but where the water is deep enough for ocean-going vessels. Using a handful of the dollars he carried in the pockets of his handsome Zairean tunic, Jimfish bought tickets on a cargo ship bound for the dark lady's country of Liberia and they sailed to the coast, at Moanda, where the mighty Congo river meets the Atlantic Ocean face to face.

CHAPTER 17

Monrovia, Liberia, 1991

On arriving in the port of Monrovia, the travellers disembarked and the dark lady was overcome with happiness to be back in her own country, which years before, as the innocent fiancée of the wicked Minister of Mines in Zaire, she had been forced to leave.

'Welcome to Liberia, where peace prevails and we indigenous people run our own affairs!' she told Jimfish and Lunamiel. 'How far we have come, and how long ago it seems, when we were very like your own appalling country, where a tiny group of white bigots whips black people into line, when they don't go about shooting them dead.'

She'd barely finished speaking when the characteristic tick-tick of heavy automatic fire around the port sent them scurrying for safety behind a line of burnt-out army trucks. They seemed to have arrived in a war zone. Fighters were everywhere: firing, falling, cheering and dying.

Crouching near them was a military man covered in medals. He was watching the battle with great calm, as if he had seen a lot of this fighting before and was undismayed. Catching sight of him, their friend was overjoyed.

'The good Lord has saved us! Here is my uncle, one of my very own Krahn people from my home village. He's a soldier and he will know what this violence means.'

When she introduced her friends, Jimfish was embarrassed to hear himself and Lunamiel identified as South Africans, knowing how detested his compatriots were throughout the continent. It was scant comfort that he wasn't white or any other colour anyone could put a name to; while Lunamiel, though beautifully bronzed, was not quite coppery enough to pass for brown.

He needn't have worried. Having embraced his niece, the military man introduced himself as Brigadier Washington Truman Roosevelt and he shook Jimfish's hand warmly, saying how delighted he was to have another South African in his country.

'Come more often and come in numbers! Liberia needs you. We're in the middle of a cruel civil war that began earlier this year and gets worse every day. Thousands have been killed in the fighting.'

'But who is fighting?' cried the dark lady, distraught at the news that her once-peaceful country was again at war.

'That's complicated,' said her uncle. 'The army of President Doe – known as the Armed Forces of Liberia is fighting the National Patriotic Front of Liberia, which is the private army of an ambitious young warlord called Charles Taylor. Recently a third group, led by Prince Johnson, an even more ambitious warlord, calling themselves the

Independent National Patriotic Front of Liberia, split away from the second group and joined the war.'

'What exactly are these groups fighting for?' Jimfish asked. 'Land or treasure or power?'

The brigadier considered this question. 'Those are some of the aims, perhaps, but for the most part each side simply wants to kill as many of its enemies as possible. Sometimes I think it is the only employment open to men around here. War gives them a job, a gun and a life. Well, at least for a while.'

Watching the pitched battles going on between fighters who thought nothing of decimating a line of attackers, slicing off the hands of prisoners or decapitating their enemies with enormous knives, Jimfish was struck by the impeccable logic of the brigadier's reply.

'Then at the end of the day, will the side with most men still standing be the winner?'

The brigadier shook his head. 'At the end of the day no one will be left standing. What we are seeing is not so much war as a long-drawn-out national suicide. That's why I'm delighted to see you. We think very highly of the fighting skill of South Africans. I've seen how good they are in neighbouring Sierra Leone, which is in the throes of a civil war every bit as bloody as ours. Working there is an outfit called Superior Solutions, and it's full of South Africans. They're in great demand in many countries north of Limpopo, where their professionalism and their willing-ness to work for whoever pays them best is widely welcomed. Their slogan is: "To African problems we bring Superior Solutions." It's the latest form of out-sourcing.

They supply men and materiel and do the fighting; in return, we pay them in diamonds. It's the perfect marriage.'

Jimfish struggled to come to terms with what he heard. 'I thought everyone hated the idea of working with South Africans?'

The brigadier shrugged. 'At one time, yes. Of course, a lot of collaboration with the regime down south still went on. But it was always hidden. Nowadays it's open season and any strong man worth his secret bank account, who feels a little uneasy about his rival or is in trouble with his people, is ready to cut a deal with the old enemy.'

Jimfish was nonplussed. 'What can have happened to bring about this great change?'

Now it was the brigadier who looked surprised. 'Where on earth have you been that you haven't heard the news?'

'In Zaire,' Jimfish and Lunamiel told him.

'Ah well, now I understand. That hellhole is as mad and as bad and as far from the real world as ever it was when the Belgians ran it – if not further,' said the brigadier. 'Let me give you news from home. After twenty-seven years behind bars Nelson Mandela has been freed and everyone knows he will be the next President of South Africa. Instead of being polecats and pariahs, South Africans are fast becoming hot property. Their armaments, muscle, money and business acumen – personified in the military advisors of Superior Solutions – find willing buyers up and down the continent. In fact, if you would consider, my dear Jimfish, joining in this civil war of ours, you would be invaluable. I would promote you to colonel in my own regiment and pay you in diamonds as large as sugar lumps.'

But here he was interrupted. A small boy with a very large gun was waving to him and the brigadier told them he'd have to finish the conversation later.

'There is a fourth force fighting in this civil war. My own. Now I must run. My troops are waiting.'

CHAPTER 18

With that, Brigadier Washington Truman Roosevelt slipped away, and when he appeared again at the head of his troops he was a changed man. He had taken off all his clothes except for his laced-up leather boots, and he was leading a squadron of children, most of them boys, who could not have been more than twelve years old. They were armed with AK-47s or rocket-propelled grenades, or manned machine guns mounted on pickup trucks, and were wailing and shrieking like demented banshees as they advanced fearlessly on the enemy.

But it was their fancy dress that was as frightening as their firepower. These children might have been the drunken guests at an insane wedding party or a ghoulish college graduation or Halloween frolic: some wore bridal gowns, others tiaras, wedding veils, mortar boards or they sported purple and pink fright wigs. But there was nothing theatrical about their weapons or their fighting abilities. These boys played real warfare like a deadly game that leaked blood, cheering and whooping at every kill, whipped into a frenzy that gave them, in their tatty wedding finery and garish fright wigs, the look of an army of maddened, murderous midgets.

Jimfish and Lunamiel were still shaking when, some time later, the brigadier returned to the safety of the line of burnt-out trucks. He was once again dressed in his military uniform and could not have been further from the naked commander in laced-up leather boots leading his children into battle. He seemed rather amused by the confusion he had caused in the minds of the South Africans.

'My brigade, as you see, is made up of children, and young minds need something to focus on. I lead my boys on what we call magical military manoeuvres. I use special charms in action, the secret of which I am not at liberty to share with you, but these protect me from enemy fire.'

'Surely it's not a good thing to teach children to kill?' Jimfish asked him.

The brigadier thought this over. 'Children need a role in life. They want direction and training. I provide those things. Where would these kids find a job if I didn't take them in my Small Boys Unit? Where would they learn the skills needed to get ahead in Liberia today, except by following Brigadier Bare-Butt, as they like to call me? I teach them to handle a gun and to kill. Essential skills. And career opportunities. Promising fighters can become cooks to the officers, or drivers and bodyguards. And we never discriminate on grounds of sex. Some of the best fighters in my Small Boys Unit are actually girls. It's the wigs that confuse the issue. The more talented girls have an advantage over the boys because they become companions to the big brass in my brigade.'

'Why do you take off your clothes?' Jimfish asked Brigadier Bare-Butt.

'Tactics. In my role as magical leader I mix the military with the mystical. And if you want to turn enemy bullets to water, then not just any old magic will do. It takes a very powerful sacrifice.'

'Sacrifice?' Lunamiel trembled.

'Before a battle we choose one of the boys,' said the brigadier, 'cut him into pieces and dine on his heart. All those lucky enough to belong to the Small Boys Unit know the ropes. We choose for the sacrifice a boy who has not been fighting well. It strengthens morale in the unit and concentrates the minds of the others.'

Jimfish thought this over. He recalled in Matabeland how the North Korean-trained troops of General Jesus slaughtered anyone they assumed were dissidents, as well as the old, the ill and the young. He remembered how remote the dead looked; how so much noise and the heat of the killing gave in return such pale, cold, still results. But he had never seen children trained to kill adults. How he missed, all over again, the counsel of Soviet Malala, who would have been able to explain to him what to make of this murderous rage, when kids as young as ten or twelve, carrying automatic rifles taller than themselves, led by a stark-naked man, slaughtered all who opposed them. Was this another example of the rage that stoked the fires of the lumpenproletariat? And which side of history were these hopped-up young killers on?

He was so confused that he blurted out a question to Brigadier Bare-Butt, which he quickly regretted.

'Surely, sir, you don't believe all that mumbo-jumbo about magic charms turning bullets to water?'

Brigadier Bare-Butt bristled. 'Mumbo-jumbo? It's clear to me that you understand very little of the traditions of Liberia. Ever since the Americans arrived in our country we've been a highly religious people and faith is our lodestar. Without this firm spiritual foundation my boys would not be the terrifyingly effective fighters they are. My sacred duty is to fortify their belief in the arms they use and in the magic charms that protect me. So I also prescribe cocaine before a battle, with marijuana to follow, by way of rest and relaxation.'

But then the brigadier was called away to lead another charge of his Small Boys Unit. His niece suggested to Jimfish and Lunamiel that they all move on to her home village and Jimfish was very happy to do so, as the cries of the dying unnerved him, and, besides, there was something in the way the brigadier stared at Lunamiel that he did not like.

His suspicions were confirmed before long. No sooner had they arrived in the Krahn village, where the family of Lunamiel's loyal and kindly attendant had their home, than she whispered to Lunamiel that the brigadier was deeply in love with her and wished to marry her.

'I am very flattered,' Lunamiel answered bravely, 'but I love Jimfish and want one day to marry him.'

'You must be crazy!' her servant told her. 'You're a girl from a traditional, white South African family with the highest ethnic requirements. Your father was a policeman, dedicated to keeping everyone safely locked in the prisons of their skins. Your mother employed so many maids she put one to work on each hand when her fingernails needed attention. And yet you dream of marrying a man as pale as a fish in some lights, pale prawn-pink in others, and he sometimes shows an unearthly blue tinge. A fellow so mixed in colour it sent your father wild when he found you two entangled on a red picnic rug in the garden. What would your poor family say to your decision to marry him?'

'In the first place,' Lunamiel declared, 'my mother and father are no more. They were blown to pieces by the liberation army, while at their prayers. Besides, we now know that everything is changed for the best in the new South Africa. Nelson Mandela is out of jail. From now on, race won't matter, colour won't count, black, white and brown people will be equal and none of us will ever be made to live in the prisons of our skins.'

'If you believe that then you are even more foolish than I imagined,' her attendant told her. 'Old delusions don't vanish because a government changes. Far from fading away, I'd say that the colour you happen to be in the new South Africa may count for even more than it did before.'

But she could see that Lunamiel did not believe her and so she thought of another plan. A most interesting item of news from the port of Monrovia reached her and she went immediately to Jimfish.

'Remember I warned you that the gendarmerie in Zaire would be after you?' she said. 'Not for shooting the Minister of Education – no problem there – but for the death of the American agent. Well, I've heard alarming news. The CIA is after you now. One of their agents is in this country to hunt you down. Get out while you can or you're a dead man!'

'But what will happen to my darling Lunamiel?' Jimfish asked.

'Haven't I brought you out of Zaire? And looked after Lunamiel?' the dark lady asked. 'She will manage, rest assured. She's a white South African raised to believe God is on her side. Like my uncle, the brigadier, who believes that going into battle stark naked, but for his boots and his AK-47, turns enemy bullets to water. Faith drives out fear. But all you have, poor Jimfish, is a talent for attracting disaster, and this time you must save yourself.'

CHAPTER 19

With a heavy heart at abandoning Lunamiel, and reckoning that the best way of escape was by sea, Jimfish made his way back to the port of Monrovia. But the ships that had been docked in the harbour were gone or had anchored out at sea. The reasons were soon clear: the fighting around the port was even more intense than it had been when Jimfish arrived. The army of Samuel Doe continued to hurl itself at the fighters of Charles Taylor, who were in turn assailed by the forces of Prince Johnson, while all sides were harried by the bewigged Small Boys Unit of Brigadier Bare-Butt, who led his juvenile killers with his customary naked aplomb.

But now a new force, uniformed and disciplined, seemed to be trying to reduce the intensity of the fighting between the various combatants. However, the response of those they wished to help was to shoot at these peacekeepers. So murderous was the firefight that Jimfish once again found himself crouching behind the same line of burnt-out army trucks where he had met Brigadier Bare-Butt on his arrival in Monrovia.

Also sheltering there was a small man with a large pistol at his waist. Even without taking into account his crew cut, his military fatigues and his very good dental work, Jimfish knew instantly this must be the American assassin sent to hunt him down. He was on the point of reaching for his revolver in its python-skin holster when the other man held out his hand in the friendliest way and introduced himself.

'Privileged to make your acquaintance, Mr Jimfish, sir. Can't tell you my real name. If I did, I'd have to shoot you. Why don't you call me John Doe? No relation to the man holed up over there.' He nodded his chin towards the port buildings, where the fighting was most intense. Seeing the puzzlement on Jimfish's face, he patted his arm soothingly. 'You thought I was here to conclude your career conclusively, as we call such assignments back at the office. Right you are. I won't deny we considered that option. We were sure real mad at you when you popped our guy in the palace of the Great Leopard down Gbadolite way. Our man had the job of funnelling arms, along with bushels of bucks, to Marshal Mobutu, as well as fixing visits for our politicians who fancied a bit of R&R in the court of the King of the Congo. But looking at your record, we got to wondering – who exactly *is* this guy? How is it that, sure as shooting, wherever Jimfish shows up everything falls apart?'

Jimfish blushed at compliments so far from the truth. If the really serious question in life was how to arrive on the right side of history, then he felt further than ever from finding an answer. All he had learnt so far had been that those who claimed to have reached that blessed destination had got there by wading through blood.

Jimfish pointed to the orderly, uniformed troops, who, despite being attacked by all sides, were not firing back. 'Whose forces are those?'

'Peacekeepers,' John Doe said. 'Troops from Ghana, Nigeria, Sierra Leone, Gambia and Guinea. They're supposed to stop the fighting.'

'They don't seem to be making much difference.' Jimfish was more puzzled than ever.

'No peace to keep,' said John Doe. 'Basically, they take note of the slaughter, about which they can do zilch. They go through the motions, so the worldwide, bleeding-heart, Something-Must-Be-Done brigade feels a bit better. But the fighters who back Charles Taylor or Prince Johnson or Brigadier Bare-Butt are all in a race, see? Whoever gets to bump off the present leader, President Doe, also gets to run Liberia. Fair enough, you might say. Leave it to the market, and may the best warlord win. But it's not that easy. We also have a dog in this fight. After all, who was it who founded this goddam country? Settled it with our freed slaves, named it and gave it American values? The rule's always been you don't get to be Numero Uno round here without our say-so. When Master Sergeant Samuel Doe blew away President Tolbert ten years back it took us ages to make Liberia safe for American interests once again. If Samuel Doe now goes and gets his career conclusively concluded, by one warlord or another, our years of hard work go down the tubes. So I need President Doe alive and in one piece. We've got too much riding on this for him to let the side down now.'

'But how will you find him?' Jimfish asked.

The American pointed to the port buildings. 'Over there is the peacekeepers' HQ. Word has it Sam Doe ducked into those buildings early today to talk about a truce.'

'Then he's safe.' Jimfish was relieved.

The American shook his head. 'Alive, maybe. Safe, no. And neither for very long unless we find him first.'

When the fighting slackened, the American signalled to Jimfish and together they made a run for the port buildings.

CHAPTER 20

Moving from room to room, they found scattered cartridge casings and puddles of blood, which John Doe studied as a skilled tracker checks the spoor of the game he is hunting. These traces led to the first floor, where they came across the bodies of several smartly dressed men.

'Doe's cabinet ministers,' said John Doe.

Jimfish stared at the bodies. 'How can you be sure?'

'They follow a pattern, these coups – and I can read the signs real easy. God knows we've backed enough of them.' With a casual toe the American turned over the victims. 'See their thousand-dollar suits and Italian shoes? The sparkly stuff – Rolexes, rings, ear-studs – that's been stripped. I'd say all government people are being wasted. That tells me they're at stage two of the coup.'

'More bloodshed?' Jimfish wondered.

'Blood's done. Next comes electioneering,' said John Doe. 'Coups get legal heft by calling out the voters. Turns the killing kosher. Let's head for Party Headquarters. Have you noticed: the fighting's stopped?'

Jim was aware of the eerie silence. 'That's good.'

The American shook his head. 'I like gunfire. That way I know what the bastards are up to.'

'How do we find the President?' Jimfish asked.

'We follow the corpses,' said John Doe.

The bodies of ministers in their fancy suits pointed the way like broken arrows. As they passed the headquarters of the opposing factions Jimfish was fascinated by the posters plastered on the walls touting election promises and platforms. Charles Taylor was running on his record and his message was simple: 'I KILLED YOUR MA. I KILLED YOUR PA. VOTE FOR ME OR I'LL KILL YOU TOO!' Brigadier Bare-Butt's posters depicted the man himself, wearing only his signature boots and AK-47, above his election promise: 'GIVE ME YOUR SON. GIVE ME YOUR DAUGHTER. I TURN THE ENEMY'S BULLETS TO WATER!' Prince Johnson, by contrast, seemed refreshingly modest. He ran no posters, made no promises. But then he did not need to. In the street outside his headquarters, stripped naked on a steel bedstead and stretched out on his back, lay the body of President Samuel Doe. Both his ears were missing. Around him a ring of grinning soldiers, waving automatic weapons, were posing for photographs.

To Jimfish it was the quintessential portrait of the times: preening soldiers pointing bayonets at a dead man. He was struck by the need to record these things on film, to get your commemorative, take-home party snap while posing beside a human being you'd stripped, shot, mutilated and tortured. To frolic around a corpse in rollicking good spirits, as if you were at a party or a picnic. If this was what happened when the rage of the lumpenproletariat turned to rocket fuel, then Jimfish felt less and less sure he wanted any part of it.

Across the street from the earless, naked ex-President on the iron bedstead was a makeshift cinema fashioned from tarpaulin and corrugated iron; people were watching a movie that must have been shot earlier, because it showed Samuel Doe still very much alive, stark naked and in a state of some distress, which was not particularly surprising since his right ear was missing. Prince Johnson, the rebel commander gave an order and a soldier sawed off President Doe's left ear, while a nurse from the warlord's team, suspecting her chief might be under some strain, gently massaged Prince Johnson's neck, while he sipped a beer. The audience loved the ear scene. Very much as the crowds in the Budapest Square had been transfixed by the execution of Nicolae and Elena Ceauşescu, these lookers-on in a street cinema projected themselves into the movie of a murder and could not get enough of it.

But then, Jimfish asked himself, was he much better? Hadn't he shot dead an American secret agent, as well as a Minister of Education, without so much as blinking? He longed to be able to talk to Soviet Malala and to ask him: 'Isn't it this joy, these wild good spirits we feel in cruelty, rather than rage or the dream of landing on the right side of history, that marks out our singular species for what we are: homicidal apes who kill their own kind with delight and afterwards write moral commandments? And which is more disgusting – the gleeful killer or the guilty sermonizer?'

'I guess there's a symmetry to this,' his American friend remarked. 'After all, when Samuel Doe rubbed out his predecessor President Tolbert he also felt he had to bump off everyone who had worked with Tolbert. Looks like history is repeating itself. Anyone close to that naked guy on the bed is for the chop.'

But Jimfish did not want to hear about symmetry or history. He wanted Lunamiel back. He wanted to ask Soviet Malala what good anger served if it made people cut off the ears of their presidents, drop villagers down mineshafts or toss a good man like Jagdish into the hell of the Chernobyl reactor.

In despair he closed his eyes. 'Everything I touch crumbles. Everywhere I go, the worst happens.'

'Don't you believe it, boy, you're a marvel,' said his American friend. 'Back at my office in the US we have a name for what happens when you turn up some place – we call it the Jimfish Effect. We ran your file and we were amazed.

'Back six years ago, in 1984, you were just a fishy fellow in this little port on the coast of South Africa. Adopted, acquired, borrowed – who knows? – by some old fisherman. Next you get to meet your new President, Piet the Weapon, and wham-bam! there are bombs going off in churches and bars and supermarkets across your country and funerals all the time. Seems South Africa is set for a big fat race war.

'But you've moved on. It's 1985, you're in Zimbabwe where Bob Mugabe is the liberator, redeemer and dear leader. Except, that is, in Matabeleland, where Bob's boys, taught to kill by Kim Il-sung, are shooting the locals at a steady rate and dropping them down mineshafts.

'A year later, 1986, you hit Uganda and, just as you steam into town, President Milton Obote is on his way out. Second time around. He got booted out by Idi Amin first time round. Then he came back when Big Dada got the chop, but now Milt's headed south again. Only this time he takes every last cent in the Ugandan treasury with him.

'On you zip to Ukraine, where the Chernobyl nuclear plant blows up and the Soviets go damn near broke putting a lid on it. All this in the same year! Then Moscow packs you off to a Siberian prison camp for being an American spy. If only! Our agents were predicting Soviet power still had decades to go when the place was actually on its last legs.

'After a few years in the gulag, the Russians send you to East Berlin. Bad move. It's November, 1989 – and guess what? When Jimfish flies in, the Berlin Wall falls down. Job done, you head for Romania and before you can say "the Genius of the Carpathians" Nicolae and Elena Ceauşescu get their careers conclusively concluded.

'Do you stop there? Not a damn. In 1990 it's Zaire, where you blow away the Minister of Education, along with one of our guys for good measure. You scoot pretty fast, but your effect lingers. The Great Leopard suddenly turns democrat. And it's all down to how you helped him see things, when the Ceauşescus got it in the neck. Instead of killing his opponents, Marshal Mobutu suddenly lets opposition parties set up shop. Everyone gets to vote, one party replaces the other, but it makes next to no damn difference in the end because the Great Leopard takes all. We've tried for years to get him to learn that trick.

'And now, here you are in Liberia. And what's happening? President Doe and his ministers are toast, and crazy civil war is tearing the place to bits. How do you do it, Jimfish? You're a force of history. A one-man weapon of mass destruction. Why not work for us? We could use a little of whatever it is you've got.'

Jimfish said, politely but firmly, that he was done with history, with blood and violence.

But John Doe would not take no for an answer. 'Not sure history is done with you. President Doe is dead. The hunt is on for those close to him. You could be next.'

'I never knew him,' said Jimfish.

'It's who you hang out with,' said John Doe. 'Samuel Doe always pushed and promoted his own Krahn tribe. You've been an honoured guest in his village. Get out fast or you're dead meat.'

'Where can I go?' Jimfish asked. 'There are no ships in the harbour and the roads are full of soldiers.'

His American friend nodded. 'Why not spend time in our embassy compound? Safe enough. See it this way – the Soviets are down the tube, we're the only superpower still standing. The world's a dangerous place. Help us in our mission to spread democracy and dignity around the globe.'

Jimfish was very wary. 'How would I do that?'

'We're planning a small operation in Somalia very soon,' said the other.

The prospect made Jimfish feel quite weak. 'Thank you, but no,' he said. 'It sounds like an invasion.'

'This time it's going to be different,' John Doe promised. 'We will march into Mogadishu with the stars and stripes flying high and the Somali people will cheer us as liberators.'

'What are you liberating them from?' Jimfish asked.

'From themselves, from poverty, hunger, Communism,' said John Doe. 'Somalia had the usual dictator who killed his people in the usual way. But he hopped into a tank the other day and headed south, taking along much of the loot from the national bank. They used to be funded by the Soviets, but they got divorced and now they have nothing. Somalia's a basket case.'

'Then what can you do?' Jimfish was increasingly puzzled.

'It's a basket case with big advantages,' his American friend explained. 'In Liberia and Sierra Leone different factions and tribal groups fight each other to the death. But Somalis are the same stock, follow one religion, speak the same language. They're one big family and they really ought to get along just fine.'

'Then maybe you should leave them alone?'

John Doe patted him on the shoulder. 'Somalia needs us, Jimfish. In go the marines, followed by the aid agencies. We'll supply food, medicine, movies and love.'

'It still sounds like an invasion,' said Jimfish.

'"Intervention" is the word. Humanitarian. Surgical. Brief. Targeted at the starving, the sick and all who yearn for democracy. And you have a very special role to play.'

There was something about this cheery reassurance that worried Jimfish.

'What will that be?'

The American became quite choked up. 'We're calling our mission "Operation Restore Hope". Hope needs a harbinger . . .'

Jimfish had no idea what 'harbinger' meant, but it had a good ring to it. And so did 'hope'. After having been a one-man weapon of mass destruction, whose arrival in half a dozen countries, though it may not have caused, had certainly coincided with sadness and savagery, it would be a relief – Jimfish felt – to be a harbinger of hope.

CHAPTER 21

Sierra Leone, 1992

The helicopter lifted into the powder-blue, empty African sky, en route to Somalia. His American friend carried a linen bag on his lap, occasionally patting it soothingly as if it were a baby. He was very cheerful.

'Lovely little bird, this Blackhawk. Some really gorgeous killing features. Nothing flying today is quite like it. We're going to make one stop on our way. I need to see a man about a war going on right next door in Sierra Leone. Just a hop and a skip away.'

He opened the white linen bag and showed Jimfish what looked like a heap of grubby stones or chips of gravel.

'Rough diamonds. In this neck of the woods diamonds are the fuel everything runs on.'

'Rocket fuel?' Jimfish wondered.

'Any kind of fuel you care to name,' said John Doe. 'That's the beauty of these babies. The war in Sierra Leone is paid for with these dirty little stones that polish up real neat, look good in candlelight. They change hands amongst guys who often don't have any hands, because slicing them off is a big thing for fighters on all sides.'

Jimfish was horrified. 'That's a crime, surely?'

John Doe nodded. 'Worse, it's dumb. If you want a good conflict currency, why not go for something grown-up like the dollar? But in West Africa diamonds are a warlord's best friend. Everyone wants to get their hands on these babies. Even if they've got no hands.'

A couple of hours later the Blackhawk put down in Freetown and a jeep with driver and an escort of white soldiers met the chopper.

'My, but we're honoured,' said John Doe. 'Seems the Commandant has sent his own jeep for us. What gives? Let me have a little one-to-one with the driver.'

When he came back to Jimfish he was shaking his head in amazement.

'Apparently the Commandant's a hard-nosed bastard, all neck and no brains, but the driver says he wants to meet you. Alone.'

'Who are these white soldiers?' Jimfish asked as they drove into Freetown.

John Doe urged him to watch his language. 'Civil contractors is what we call them. Or security consultants. Or enhanced assets. Or strategic suppliers. *Never* soldiers.'

As they reached the town, John Doe hopped out of the jeep. 'So long, Jimfish. Good luck!'

Jimfish was uneasy at being left alone. 'Where are you going?'

'The Commandant wants to see you on your own. I'll be talking loot with a local warlord.'

'You talk to warlords?' Jimfish was shocked.

'Constructive engagement,' said John Doe. 'You have a good day now. Meet you back at the Commandant's office.'

Have a good day! How could he do that when he remembered Lunamiel, abandoned in Liberia, the plaything of Brigadier Bare-Butt. The more he saw of the world, the less he understood. Worse still, what he did understand was so crazy, so cruel, that none of the lessons of his old teacher Soviet Malala seemed to apply; not rage nor the many sides of history, neither the lumpenproletariat, nor the settler entity. Never had he felt so confused. And the menacing silence of the white soldiers escorting him – when he asked them their names or their reasons for being in Sierra Leone – made him even more miserable. Soon he would be heading to Somalia, another country he did not know, on a humanitarian intervention he did not understand, on a mission he did not like the sound of – not one little bit. And what, for heaven's sake, was a harbinger of hope?

The jeep dropped Jimfish at the door of a large hotel which had been badly damaged by rocket fire, like so many of the buildings in Freetown. He was led into what was once the manager's office and there sat a man in military khaki, wearing a cap laced with gold braid and large sunglasses, who sported a bushy beard as broad as a shovel. The armed escort saluted their chief, who returned the salute, and this went on for some time before the escort was dismissed.

Jimfish felt more wretched than ever, faced by the man in the gold braid. What was he to say to this imposing personage? As John Doe had warned, he did look all neck; it was as broad as a baobab trunk, climbing from his tunic collar up into his heavily gold-encrusted cap. But when the Commandant pulled a bottle out of the desk drawer and asked him if he'd like a brandy and Coke, Jimfish's heart leaped. It was such a stroke of luck he hardly dared to believe what he had heard, but the man's accent was unmistakeable.

'Are you perhaps South African?'

The other nodded so hard his beard gave off a breeze. 'Born and bred and proud of it.'

'My countryman!' Jimfish embraced him. 'One of us!'

The other extricated himself and gave Jimfish a careful look. 'Up to a point, maybe.'

'Where exactly are you from?' Jimfish asked eagerly.

'From little Port Pallid, on the Indian Ocean,' said the soldier.

Jimfish knew suddenly who he was and his heart blazed with happiness.

'What blessed luck! You're Deon Arlow, brother of Lunamiel.'

The other nodded. 'Commandant Arlow, if you don't mind. And now that I cast my mind back, aren't you the fellow who was sitting, or even lying, on a red picnic rug in my father's orchard, entangled with my sister?'

'That's right!' Jimfish was overjoyed, after being so long so lost in the world, to meet a fellow countryman.

'My dad got so damn furious he tried to shoot you.' Deon Arlow laughed at the memory. 'It's only natural. But you got away scot-free. Isn't that so, hey?'

So overwhelmed with delight at meeting another of his

own kind was Jimfish that he found himself nodding. After all, shooting people was what Sergeant Arlow did for a living. It was nothing personal. In fact, Jimfish felt a tiny twinge of remorse at having deprived Sergeant Arlow of doing what came so naturally. As he sat and sipped his brandy and Coke he felt a surge of South African camaraderie so strong he almost apologized to Deon Arlow for having got away scot-free.

CHAPTER 22

Deon Arlow poured Jimfish another brandy and Coke.

'I'm the first to say those were mad times. Race, colour, blood and tribe drove us crazy. But that's all behind us now. I'm so proud that my sister Lunamiel was at the forefront of this push into Africa.'

'As I remember,' said Jimfish, 'you traded her for mineral rights in Zaire.'

'Exactly. A brave move at the time, I can tell you. Who says white guys can't adapt and reach out to our African brothers? Commerce not conflict is the way to go. Since we embedded my sister in Zairean high society I've opened branches in Angola, Liberia and Sierra Leone, with more deals to come.'

'And what's the name of this excellent example of commercial outreach?' Jimfish asked.

'Superior Solutions,' came the reply.

Jimfish remembered Brigadier Bare-Butt's warm greeting when they met behind the line of burnt-out army trucks during the battle for Monrovia.

'You mean you fight other people's wars – for money?'

Deon Arlow shook his head so violently his beard swung to and fro beneath his chin like a bushy pendulum.

'Not just money. We take gold, oil, dollars, platinum, rare earths, uranium yellow cake – in this case' – he pulled out a linen bag very like the one John Doe had been carrying – 'it's diamonds.'

'But then, surely, you must be mercenaries?' Jimfish was appalled.

The Commandant smiled at his naiveté. 'Mercenaries are medieval. Then came conscripts, when the worst of the fighting fell to lowly private soldiers. But the willingness to die in numbers is not what it was. The old cannon-fodder model is kaput. Replaced by the contractor paradigm. Think of us as management consultants *sans frontières*. Businessmen, not brigands. We consult, confer, clobber, console. In return, we are paid in whatever currency the dominant warlord prefers.'

Jimfish was confused by this talk of models and paradigms. 'Then who does the killing?'

The Commandant shook his head. 'Not a word we use. We contain, counter, stabilize, neutralize, pulverize. We contract to downsize the bad guys or maximize the weak. Sometimes we save innocents from being hacked to pieces by lawless soldiery. We can peacekeep or we can plaster enemy guts all over the bloody place. Outsourcing assets. More and more countries are seeing the light. The Great Leopard in Zaire, he headhunts Croat and Serb snipers to put down local uprisings at home. Makes an internal market, because Serbs and Croats hate each other and so they compete on kill-rates.'

The Commandant walked over to the map of Africa on the wall and tapped Pretoria. 'Here's the question I asked myself when I started out: why look abroad for talents we've got at home? For decades our own government spent buckets of blood and bags of treasure fighting black terrorists – and most whites were pretty damn happy with that. Then, just last year, without a word of warning, our new President caves in, signs a peace treaty and tells us to jump into bed with the enemy. Where does that leave lots of young guys – white and black – who've never known anything but war and more war? If they can't kick it, eat it, shoot it or screw it they haven't a clue what to do. That's when I saw a gap in the market. Our rulers may have thrown in the towel and settled for peace, but plenty of other rogue regimes – all over Africa – are in the market, looking to do what we did so well. Only they don't have our skills or our arms industry.'

The Commandant marched Jimfish to the window and pointed to the white soldiers who had escorted him from the chopper, now grabbing a bit of shut-eye in the shade.

'I said to myself: "Deon, my boy, there must be a rich niche for a mobile fighting force with terrific weapons and a civilizing mission." I started in a small way over in Angola, cleaning out rebel strongholds. And now I have more work than I can handle. You want a coup backed – or bust? You want your current dictator safe – or dead? You need the folks over the hill to be conclusively terminated? Look no further. Superior Solutions has the plan to suit your treasury. Right now, I'm fixing a deal with interested parties, right here in Freetown.' He poured Jimfish another large brandy and Coke and raised his glass. 'Here's to Superior Solutions: a proudly South African company.'

Jimfish felt it was only polite to join in the toast, before asking Deon Arlow a question of vital importance.

'And what can you tell me of your sister Lunamiel?'

The Commandant shrugged: 'I hear she's been grabbed by that demented Liberian mystic Brigadier Bare-Butt. I'm no racist. All's fair in love and war, etcetera. But between you and me I'd love to whizz across the border into Liberia and nail the brigadier's ugly backside to a baobab.'

'I'll come with you!' cried Jimfish. 'We can take the helicopter and rescue my Lunamiel and then we'll get married.'

'Hold it right there!' Deon Arlow was furious. 'What did you just say? My sister is a white girl, one hundred and fifty per cent pure-as-snow European and proud of it. Back home in Port Pallid my late father made me swear I would never ever let his daughter – an Aryan to the nth degree – marry a black man.'

'You hold it right there!' Jimfish was himself suddenly so angry he quite surprised himself. 'Didn't you lease-lend Lunamiel on a timeshare contract to the Zairean Minister of Education?'

'That was business,' said Deon Arlow. 'Constructive engagement. It is not the same as letting my sister marry a black man.'

'Who says I'm black?' demanded Jimfish.

Deon Arlow looked him over and what he saw puzzled

him, because Jimfish really didn't look quite human. He was pale and pink in some lights or eerily ice-white or tan, but then again, at times, his skin showed a light blue tint.

'Whatever you are, you're not the right white,' he said. 'And nowadays, since we don't do the old apartheid talk any more, back in Port Pallid anyone not strictly white – and that goes for Asians, Chinese, Thais, Libyans and mixed-race guys – are formally black.'

Jimfish stood up. 'The days of dividing people by colour are over. You said so yourself. If my old teacher Soviet Malala is right about anything, he's right when he says that those who keep up the struggle will land on the right side of history. I love Lunamiel, she loves me and we want to get married.'

'Over my dead body!' Deon Arlow went for his revolver, but, like his father, he was a slow, clumsy man and Jimfish beat him to the draw, pulled his pistol from its python-skin holster and calmly shot the Commandant of Superior Solutions through the heart.

It was only when the Commandant slumped to the floor that Jimfish – faced by the ghastly truth that not only was he as violent as any other man but he had really rather enjoyed it – broke into wails of despair.

'What have I done? I hate brutality and murder! But I've already killed a government minister and an American secret agent! Now I've shot my future brother-in-law!'

Luckily, his sobs alerted John Doe, who had returned from a useful meeting with local warlords. He took one look at the scene and, being trained for this sort of thing, he knew what to do: he began stripping the dead man.

'Take off your clothes,' he instructed Jimfish, handing him the Commandant's uniform, finishing with his cap and dark glasses. Then very neatly he scissored off Deon Arlow's great beard and fixed it to Jimfish's chin with duct tape.

'This is what we do next.' He handed Jimfish the dead man's bag of diamonds, assuring him they would come in useful. 'I'll fetch the Commandant's jeep and you jump in the back. Soon as they see you, the Commandant's men will snap to attention and salute. You salute in return and while all this saluting is going on, we drive away. We'll be airborne in the Blackhawk and heading for Somalia before they know what's happened.'

And so it was that Jimfish escaped from Sierra Leone, laden with diamonds, but with a heavy heart, knowing that he had once again failed to land on the right side of history.

CHAPTER 23

Mogadishu, Somalia, 1992–93

The Blackhawk floated above Mogadishu, giving Jimfish his first glimpse of Somalia, and touched down in a field outside town. John Doe seemed anxious to get away the moment he had deposited his passenger, and just before closing the hatch he shouted a rapid briefing on his role as a harbinger.

'Restore hope – that's us. Harbinger – that's you. Surgical strikes. Food aid. Votes for all. Mission accomplished. Got that? God bless!'

With that the chopper lifted into the sky and Jimfish set off to walk into the capital under the fierce January summer sun.

He had not gone far when a pickup drew level with him and for a moment he thought he was being offered a lift. Then he noticed the machine gun mounted on the truck and glowering soldiers, strung with ammunition, who demanded to know if he was an American.

Jimfish was happy he could put the record straight: 'I am a harbinger of hope.'

'Without doubt, an American,' they said, pointing their guns at him. 'Tie him up.'

Jimfish pulled out his bag of rough diamonds and offered to trade, but his captors laughed. What would they do with dirty pebbles? Jimfish explained the stones could be swapped for a fortune. They laughed again. Who would trade stones for Kalashnikovs? It was dollars they wanted, but Jimfish had none. The soldiers explained that kidnapping had become the best new Somali thing. Leveraging high-end hostages into cash. Americans were blue-chip stocks. With that they tied him up, tossed him into the back of their truck and drove into Mogadishu, firing happily at anything that moved.

The truck moved through empty, silent, potholed streets lined with billboards and plastered with pictures of a stern, uniformed soldier, whose formal title was 'Victorious Leader' and whom he took to be Siad Barre, one-time and most recent dictator of Somalia. On the left-hand side of the road the former dictator was pictured in fading posters, hanging alongside Karl Marx, Lenin and the dear leader of North Korea Kim Il-sung; he was also shown locked in a bear hug with none other than Jimfish's late acquaintance Nicolae Ceauşescu, the Genius of the Carpathians.

On the right-hand side of the road were more recent posters, showing Presidents Jimmy Carter and George Bush Senior, and Jimfish remembered John Doe telling him that the Americans had replaced the Russians in supplying the dictator's need for cash and arms.

As the pickup bounced over Mogadishu's dusty, potholed roads Jimfish was once again filled with wonder at how effortlessly people reversed positions.

Seeing Nicolae Ceauşescu's face brought back to him the show trial of the dictator and his wife in Târgovişte; and how long-serving lieutenants of Ceauşescu's iron rule, abruptly and unhesitatingly switched from being life-long patriarchs of the Communist Party into proud fighters for freedom by firing squad.

Clearly, this was what sensible, pragmatic people did. Hadn't the redoubtable Robert Mugabe once gone to war to liberate his people from colonial bondage only to cheer the shooting of those who mistakenly took their freedom at face value? The liberator turned liquidator showed adaptability of a high degree.

And what of those armed guards he had seen at the Berlin Wall as it was falling down? So ready to shoot on sight anyone crossing the wall on, say, Tuesday, yet on Wednesday, calmly helping people through the breaches made by the woodpeckers with their chisels. Was this not the acme of pragmatism?

In Liberia, when Master Sergeant Samuel Doe murdered President William Tolbert, together with all his ministers to become the new President, he was demonstrating his talent, not for criminal cruelty, but for robust common sense. Samuel K. Doe, in turn, had been murdered by Prince Johnson, in about the time it takes to sink a Budweiser, setting off a race to rule Liberia amongst those warlords still standing. Which of their election promises would speak most winningly to Liberians as they were frogmarched into the voting booths? Would it be

Prince Johnson, who had carved up the late President on camera and marketed the home movie? Or Charles Taylor, running on his record of killing the mothers and fathers of his compatriots and ready to do the same to any of their children who made the wrong choice. Or would the winner be the dark horse, Brigadier Bare-Butt and his horde of hopped-up, bewigged boys, one of whom turned into the team breakfast before each battle? Hard to say.

Oh, where was Soviet Malala now? Jimfish wanted to tell him he was wrong. If this is how things were, then he no longer believed in rage and he did not care whether or not he arrived on the right side of history. If this was what adaptability meant, then he would rather die, and he said so to the soldiers as they were hauling him out of the back of the truck.

That was something they could very well offer him, they assured him, but first they would use him to set the floor price in living hostages. It was all a question of testing and trusting the market. If it turned out, when they had collected more prisoners, that they got almost as much for a dead American, then they might execute their captives and settle for a lower margin on larger volumes. With that they flung Jimfish into a cell and left him to his misery.

But he was not alone. Sitting on a bunk watching him closely was a tall fellow with a good head of hair.

'The men who have locked us up – what do they want?' Jimfish wondered. 'I offered them diamonds, but they weren't interested.'

'In a civil war there is always only one good convertible currency. In my war, dollars didn't work, nor did British pounds. For bribes or ransoms or customs fees it had to be German Deutschmarks.'

'Where was your war?' Jimfish asked him.

'Hard to say,' said his fellow prisoner with a sad smile.

'You can't have a war without a country to have it in,' said Jimfish. 'That stands to reason.'

'We don't bother much with reason where I come from,' said the other. 'Let's just say I had a country once, but it went away.'

Jimfish had to laugh. 'Where on earth did it go?'

The melancholy man shrugged. 'Who knows? One day it was there. On all the maps, in the travel brochures, available on package tours. But the next time I looked, it was gone.'

CHAPTER 24

Jimfish was baffled. Maybe the man was mad. Though, looking at him, what his fellow prisoner showed was a great and sombre calmness, as if he had faced some terrible fate and accepted it, but what he had faced was so depressing he simply could not talk about it. So he spoke in riddles.

Jimfish pressed him. 'But surely, strictly speaking, you must be *someone* from *somewhere*?'

'Strictly speaking, I'm Zoran the Serb, from Belgrade,' said the sad man with the good head of hair. 'I was a serving soldier in what was once the Yugoslav National Army. Created by a man called Tito, who made a country called Yugoslavia. I'm still a Tito man. To hear what they say about him these days, you'd think Tito wasn't a Croatian genius who kept Yugoslavia in one piece. No, he was another Hitler. And this from idiots who want only certified Serbs in Serbia and kosher Croats in Croatia and model Muslims in Sarajevo. Right down to the tribal wire, in every pathetic little Balkanette born from ex-Yugoslavia.

Each run by ex-Communists turned chauvinists, like Tuđjman in Croatia and Milošević in Serbia – savage sectarians who worship village gods.

'Once upon a time I lived in a big, joined-up country where you never had to be, strictly speaking, anyone at all. Borders didn't count. We all spoke Serbo-Croat. My sister married a Slovene, my aunt was Macedonian, my grandfather came from Montenegro and married his Bosnian wife in Kosovo. Wherever in the Federation you were born, from Dubrovnik to Nis, Pristina to Skopje, you were a Yugoslav. Until it blew up.'

'Who blew it up?' Jimfish asked.

'We did. It started when the Slovenes wanted to leave Yugoslavia, and I was sent to fight them. It wasn't much of a war and they won – or, maybe, we just let them go. We didn't see what was coming. Overnight they ditched the old Yugoslav dinar for the German Deutschmark, threw out the Serbo-Croat dictionary and told everyone that Slovenia was the new Switzerland. It was hard to keep a straight face. Their border crossing was a bit of rope stretched across the motorway, manned by goons with guns who called themselves customs officials, lolling in deckchairs under umbrellas advertising Malboro cigarettes, and a banner that said "Welcome to the Republic of Slovenia".

'Then came the next war; this time in Croatia. I was based in Karlovac and we rode to the front along the motorway, like commuters, ready to take the next exit to the battlefield. Sometimes we blew apart cities; other times we fought in quiet meadows, where a sniper hid in the belfry of the pretty little church across the fields. Our side shelled patients in hospitals, and their side blew up schoolkids. This was more like a real Balkan war and the Croats had form. They slaughtered Serbs in the Second World War; and they seemed keen to do it all over again. Our answer was to slaughter Croats. And when that sort of thing begins, no one is safe, because it's catchy, that old slaughter music. In no time all – in Bosnia, Kosovo, Macedonia – slaughter was Top of the Pops. Those things Serbs know about. Over the centuries, Belgrade has been wiped out more than a dozen times. And we also know about world war – we virtually started the First and died in droves in the Second. But this war we did not understand.'

'What brought you all the way to Africa?' Jimfish wondered.

The answer surprised him.

'I came to be enlightened. I said to myself, "If race is all the rage, if ethnic cleansing is coming soon to a mini-statelet near me, then it's time to brush up on ethnic hatred and to take a look at the way others do things." But where to start? Kashmir and the Pakistani–Indian partition? Or the Israeli–Palestine split? Belgium, where the tribes detest each other? Northern Ireland, where the sects prefer suicide? Then it came to me: who has done Balkanization better than the Balkans? South Africans! They're the champs. For decades they've been splitting their country into ethnic islands and locking up people in the prisons of race and tribe, colour and culture. Each piece of their crazy jigsaw has its own parliament, flag, president, army, borders. Everyone lives in a little hate-state where you're free to loathe the clan or the crowd down the road or across town or over the next hill.'

Jimfish did not want to say where he was from, but an unexpected surge of patriotisim made him defend his country.

'Maybe that was so in the old South Africa,' he said. 'But Nelson Mandela's out of jail now and he'll be the next President. Apartheid is dead and buried. There will be free elections, a free health service, jobs for all and a chicken in every pot every Sunday.'

Zoran the Serb shook his good head of hair in his gloomy way and waved a cautionary finger.

'If ex-Yugoslavia is anything to go by, elections just put new hats on the same old heads. In Belgrade cradle Communists turned into noisy fascists overnight. Same thing in Croatia.'

With a sinking heart, Jimfish remembered the men in hats on the roof of the Central Committee Building in Bucharest. But he felt he must defend the achievements of his country.

'In South Africa I'm sure the change will be blindingly clear.'

'Blinding, perhaps,' said Zoran, 'but clear? In ex-Yugoslavia socialists wore red and fascists went for brown. But then came the war – and we couldn't tell the difference any more. Scratch a red and he bleeds brown. And vice versa. So I decided on South Africa. Because that's where we're heading in ex-Yugoslavia.'

'You're too late.' Jimfish tried to get his cellmate to see sense. 'Those ideas are dead and gone. And so is the apostle of apartheid who invented them – Hendrik Frensch Verwoerd.'

'Maybe dead down your way, but he's alive and laughing where I come from,' said Zoran the Serb. 'My first taste of Africa was in Zaire. The Great Leopard rented a batch of us Serb and Croat sharpshooters. We lived in separate barracks, ate off separate plates with separate knives and forks, and used separate toilets. But at night, after a day in the field, we relaxed over slivovitz and spoke Serbo-Croat. We hated each other at home and fell in love in Zaire. But one day Mobutu figured out that if he wanted to modernize Zaire ballots beat bullets. Just like our man Milošević in Belgrade, he saw that elections, carefully run, are the up-to-date way to emasculate the electorate.

'Sharpshooters were suddenly surplus to requirements in Zaire. Luckily, demand for skills like mine never slackens. Siad Barre in Somalia was recruiting snipers. I'd barely signed on when the Victorious Leader climbed into a tank and headed south, taking the national bank deposits with him. No one wanted snipers any more. No money to pay them. And it's slow work, taking out one man at a time. Somali clan leaders were looking to mow down their enemies in numbers. Luckily, the Americans stepped in with RPGs and heavy automatic stuff, which the warlords love. They mount them on pickups and blow away scores of people in no time at all.'

Jimfish felt a surge of familiar confusion. 'But why should Somalis hate each other? If they're one people with one language and religion.'

Zoran the Serb smiled his sad Serbian smile. 'Ethnic

hatred is a help if you're hoping for civil war. But you don't need distinct tribes worshipping different gods to whip up a good massacre of the neighbours. A happy family can be at each other's throats quicker than you can say "ex-Yugoslavia". In Somalia it's your clan that counts. Yours against theirs. And their family feud has killed hundreds of thousands. Even more are starving. Outsiders try to help, but aid trucks get ambushed, cargo planes shot down, ships can't dock. Anyone who isn't dead is dead broke. The latest idea is to sell hostages. That's why they locked me up here. I told them: "I'm a Serb – no one wants to buy a used Yugoslav. Hell, we're worth even less than South Africans!"'

Jimfish decided it was time to tell his cellmate the truth. 'I happen to be from South Africa.'

For the first time Zoran looked quite cheered. 'Good heavens! A Serb and a South African – twin polecats of the western world and we end up in the same cell!'

Suddenly, helicopters were clattering overhead and they heard the sound of shooting. Zoran walked to the door of the cell and, to his astonishment, it opened.

'Our jailers – they've gone! What is going on? I'm getting a bad feeling.'

Jimfish was happy to reassure Zoran. 'It's very good news. They've gone to the beach. It means the Americans have landed.'

'Americans invading Somalia?' Zoran was incredulous. 'I'm getting a very bad feeling.'

'Not invading,' said Jimfish. 'Intervening. This is a humanitarian operation. The Somalis will greet them with open arms.'

'They'll open fire, more likely,' Zoran said. 'The soldiers who kidnapped us have gone hunting for high-end hostages. They don't need us bottom feeders any more.'

Jimfish was shocked at Zoran's Serbian cynicism. 'The Americans plan a short, surgical intervention. They'll feed the starving, treat the sick, shoot the warlords and leave.'

'My very bad feeling just got worse,' said Zoran. 'How do you know all this about the American plans?'

Jimfish reassured him. 'Because I am the first stage of the mercy mission – I am the harbinger of hope.'

'More like the canary in the coal mine,' said Zoran. 'Let's get out of here before the goons get back with new hostages and shoot us because they need the cell space.'

CHAPTER 25

Crouching behind a dune on the beach Jimfish and Zoran watched the first frogmen coming ashore. Under the full moon they looked in their wetsuits and flippers like walking fish. Jimfish remembered Port Pallid, the old captain who had been good to him and the great blue fish with four small legs that lived secretly in deep undersea caves, stood on its head, swam backwards and had lived on, quietly, successfully, for millions of years even though everyone was sure it was dead.

He knew, then, that it was time to go home. And yet what good would that do? When he had shot his future brother-in-law, as well as an American secret agent, plus a Minister of Education, and left his dearest Lunamiel to the mercy of a Liberian brigadier who wore nothing but his boots; and when the rage that his old teacher Soviet Malala – dead in distant Ukraine – called the rocket fuel of the lumpenproletariat had turned to tears and treachery, and his dream of arriving on the right side of history seemed as far away as ever.

As he and Zoran watched, three inflatable rubber landing craft packed with marines – their faces daubed black, carrying packs and weapons – slid out of the surf and on to the sand. It was then, as if the beach had been hit by a bolt of lightning, that night turned to day. The lights belonged to dozens of camera crews who had been waiting in the darkness.

The frogmen and the marines in their night-vision goggles were blinded by the lights and mobbed by men with important, carefully combed hair, speaking earnestly to camera. The cameras then filmed a short ceremony in which a banner was unfurled and planted on the beach; it read OPERATION RESTORE HOPE.

'What are they doing with all these cameras and lights?' Jimfish asked Zoran.

Zoran looked at his watch. 'It's prime-time evening news hour in the US. Big story: "Marines ambushed by the media in Mogadishu".'

The marines forced their way past the anchormen and began digging in, and the film crews wheeled their cameras close up and followed every spadeful of beach sand. Jimfish felt sorry for the soldiers. You land on a beach expecting to kill or be killed and, next thing you know, someone shoves a mike at you and asks if you have a special message for your girlfriend watching at home in dear old Savannah.

Next on to the beach came the amphibious vehicles, rolling up the sand dunes with their drivers yelling at cameramen to get out of the way because there was a war going on. At this point, three Somalis rushed towards the marines, holding their arms above their heads, calling, 'Don't shoot!'

They were immediately thrown down on the sand and bound by the marines, while the cameras watched.

'We are interpreters!' one of the men managed to shout, before all were gagged and turned face down in the sand.

Zoran told Jimfish to be ready to run for his life. 'Any minute now both media and marines will be ready to march on Mogadishu.'

'How can you be so sure?' Jimfish asked.

Zoran looked at his watch. 'We're probably in a commerical break right now. The networks will want to see the troops in place outside Mogadishu, ready for the next segment of the show. Straight after the ads. That's when the marines march triumphantly to the capital and the locals cheer.'

Jimfish was reassured to hear this. 'So far, so good. Mission accomplished.'

'So far, so bad and getting worse,' said Zoran. 'These poor guys haven't a clue what they will be facing. Mogadishu is a mean town: lousy with burning tyres, burning rubbish, burning hatreds. Foreign invaders with nothing to gain hunting locals with nothing to lose. A recipe for disaster. These marines are on a hiding to nowhere.'

As he predicted, film crews, marines, make-up men, hair stylists and news anchors, still talking earnestly to camera, began marching off in the direction of the capital, under the banner, OPERATION RESTORE HOPE.

'Now we grab one of those empty landing craft the marines arrived in,' said Zoran, and made for the water.

'What do we do about them?' Jimfish pointed to the

interpreters lying on the beach where the Americans had trussed them. 'Let's untie them. Then the two sides can talk to each other.'

'What good would talking do?' Zoran pushed Jimfish into one of the inflatables. 'Who wants to hear what the other side is saying? Let's get out – before this dialogue of the deaf turns into a dance of the dead.'

As they were floated into the surf, a squadron of helicopters flew overhead, heading for Mogadishu, and Jimfish was proud to be able to identify them.

'Blackhawks. Most modern killing machine around, so I'm told.'

Zoran raised his eyebrows. 'From what I've seen in ex-Yugoslavia, I'd say that prize still goes to a human with an enemy in his sights.'

Jimfish gave one last look at the three Somali interpreters still bound, gagged and kicking in the sand, and asked again if he could free them, but his words were lost as Zoran fired up the motors and they headed out to sea.

CHAPTER 26

Dar es Salaam, Tanzania, 1993

The useful thing about a large, ribbed, inflatable landing craft with two good outboard motors and loaded with plenty of extra fuel, in methodical marine fashion, was that it carried Jimfish and Zoran well down the east coast of Africa to Mombasa in Kenya, where they took on more fuel and sailed south.

During their voyage from Mogadishu the news reaching them on the landing craft's radio had been unfailingly bad. The dance of death Zoran predicted had grown into a grisly ball. Blackhawk choppers had been shot out of the sky and the mutilated bodies of American soldiers had been dragged through the streets to the cheers of onlookers. Throughout Operation Restore Hope, Somalis had gone on dying in large numbers, until eventually the Americans, along with international peacekeepers and aid agencies, declared that hope was not to be restored after all, and fled the country.

More and more often Jimfish found himself questioning the ideas of his old teacher Soviet Malala about rage, rocket fuel and the lumpenproletariat. It seemed to him as though many people were so poor and so hungry that rage was a fuel they could not afford; they were running on empty. The proletariat was not a class or category they would be allowed to join, and all they might expect was silent agony, speechless victims of the men in hats.

The two travellers arrived some days later in the port of Dar es Salaam in Tanzania, where their plan was to continue their journey by air. Their destination was South Africa, for Jimfish felt increasingly homesick and Zoran was as determined as ever to learn more about tribal homelands, ethnic enclosures and radical balkanization, as set out in the theories of Hendrik Frensch Verwoerd, of which six brand-new tribal reserves carved from the old Yugoslavia were, said Zoran, a triumphant vindication of the vision of the apostle of apartheid.

Jimfish explained time and again to the Serb that South Africa was now another sort of place where old obsessions with race and colour had been eradicated.

'That way of life is gone, it's dead and buried.'

Zoran said simply, 'Perhaps. But your past is our future. If I study what you were so good at: racial division, sectarian hatred, ethnic cleansing and triumphant tribalism, I might begin to understand what we've achieved in my ex-homeland.'

Jimfish's satchel of diamonds, once the property of the late Deon Arlow, Commandant of Superior Solutions – a proudly South African company – which had been of so little use in Mogadishu would be perfectly good exchangeable currency in peaceful Dar es Salaam. And so it was on a sun-soaked morning in the port of Dar es Salaam that Zoran the Serb set out with the satchel to buy tickets for Johannesburg.

Jimfish was keen to see something of the capital city and he walked through the streets enjoying the friendly smiles of the inhabitants. Although still sad at losing his poor Lunamiel to Brigadier Bare-Butt, he was happy to have escaped from Somalia; the sun was shining, the sky was high and blue and home felt closer and closer.

He had just turned into a narrow street behind a row of tall houses when, suddenly, he was caught fast in a net dropped dexterously over him from a high window. The net must have been attached to an articulated arm, because Jimfish was hoisted into the air and whisked through an upstairs window into a large room.

He heard someone giving careful instructions to the operator of the articulated arm.

'Raise him up into the rafters and rope him to a beam. Be careful not to touch him. Any human contact with the material will affect the potency of the magic.'

Jimfish was strung from a beam beside another man, trussed just as tightly, who told him his name was Benjamin and advised him not to struggle.

'We've been netted like fish. Better to accept our fate. This is a saleroom and it will soon be crowded with buyers.'

Jimfish struggled to understand what he was hearing. 'But what's for sale?'

'We are,' Benjamin told him. 'This is an albino auction. It's absolutely illegal, but albinos are prize catches, demand is high and we will be knocked down to eager bidders.'

'What do they want with an albino?'

Jimfish was again really angry for the second time in his life and he thrashed about in the net, which did no good at all, as his fellow captive had warned him.

'Magic,' said Benjamin sadly. 'Ridiculous as it sounds. We are like rhino horn that some swear boosts sexual potency and pay vast sums to buy. But not even the very rich can afford an entire albino. Our body parts will be auctioned off a bit at a time. Eyes, legs, fingers and toes, each bit has a reserve price.'

'Are you saying that we're to be cut into pieces?' Jimfish demanded, as anger ignited into fury and flamed within him.

'Once the sale is over, yes,' came the reply. 'Until then, they need us in one piece to keep us fresh.'

'This is barbarism!' Jimfish said.

The other man shook his head. 'The albino auction is the civilized end of the market. There are those in Tanzania and beyond who believe albinos are mystical creatures who bring luck or babies or riches or wives or husbands or cures for cancer. Better the auction room than the bounty hunters. They are really wild. You can be having a meal with your family and the hunters burst in and start hacking off legs or arms, right there and then. I'm sorry, my friend, in a few minutes we'll be knocked down to the highest bidder, then killed, then chopped up.'

'But I am not an albino,' Jimfish said. 'I am from South Africa.'

'Better not say so,' Benjamin advised. 'Foreign albinos fetch even more than the homegrown variety.'

The room was filling with buyers now. The auctioneer

opened the bidding and it soon became clear that, as his fellow captive had warned, they were being sold off, piece by piece: an eye here, an ear there, toes and fingers; a whole or half a leg. The bidding was lively and every so often the auctioneer's assistants, armed with poles, would carefully poke each net and set it spinning, to allow the bidders to get a good look at the lots on offer.

It was agony for Jimfish. True rage was welling up in him at long last, yet he was helpless, a fish caught in a net, unable to move a muscle, forced to listen as various bits of his body – from his teeth to his testicles – were briskly sold off.

It was then that a man at the back of the room joined the bidding and, to his astonished relief, Jimfish recognized Zoran the Serb. He quickly outbid all competitors, first for Jimfish, then for Benjamin. Zoran had been bidding backed by the enormous funds open to him when he exchanged a handful of the diamonds he carried, courtesy of Jimfish's late future brother-in-law. The two prize lots in the rafters were knocked down to him and the auction room rang with the hubbub that greets record sale prices.

'Does sir want them dismembered?' the auctioneer asked Zoran.

'I'll take them as they are, thank you,' Zoran told him.

'I can hear from your accent that you come from Europe,' said the auctioneer to Zoran. 'You've been very lucky to buy a pair of prime specimens – Africa's answer to the unicorn. Albinos have proven to be infallible cures for rabies, scabies, infertility, cancer, impotence, dropsy and so much more. And they're really so economical: a fingernail, an ear lobe, a single eye can work miracles. No part is wasted. Even the hair can be woven into fishing nets and guarantees a wonderful catch. Though, if you don't mind my saying so, Europeans are often sceptical of albino magic.'

'I'm from ex-Yugoslavia and, given the incredible things people in my part of the world already believe about each other, they'll be perfectly ready to buy miracle cures made from Africa's unicorn,' said Zoran.

He paid the auctioneer, called a taxi and ferried his two purchases back to the harbour. Once aboard their boat, he cut Jimfish and Benjamin free of the enfolding nets and told them how he had happened to save them.

'I was on my way to buy our airline tickets when a tout offered me the sale of a lifetime: two milky-white African unicorns. We Serbs are more used to massacres than magic and I thought "What the hell?" and followed him to the auction room. You can imagine my surprise to find you and Benjamin, each strung from the ceiling in great nets, like a catch of herring.'

Zoran was all for setting off into town once again to buy air tickets, but Benjamin warned against this: 'Jimfish is now seen as one of us and word will be out. You'll be recognized before you ever get to the airport. Once an albino, always an albino. You're worth far more dead than alive and next time you won't be so lucky. Cut up into pieces and sold.'

'Why do they kill albinos?' Jimfish asked.

'It's not seen as murder,' Benjamin told him soberly. 'They say we're ghosts already. Or our mothers slept with white men. Or we have no souls. The sooner you get away the better.'

'Why don't you escape with us?' Jimfish urged. 'We'll take our boat and sail to South Africa.'

Benjamin shook his head 'From what I hear about your country, it is full of crazy people. Racists and xenophobes. And colossal ignorance about Africa. How long would a Tanzanian albino last? I'd rather stay in my own country, even if it's no home for people like me.'

'Well, at least let me help you.' Jimfish handed him a fistful of diamonds.

Benjamin was grateful. 'I can buy some protection for a while.'

'Why not buy guns instead?' asked Zoran the Serb. 'Take the Yugoslav option: announce you can't abide anyone who doesn't belong in your ethnic group, start a war of independence and throw out anyone who isn't of your family, tribe or faith.'

'But I'm not an ethnic group,' said Benjamin. 'I just have a skin condition, resulting from the way my genes work.'

'Doesn't everyone have just skin conditions, when you get down to it?' Zoran asked. 'So set up your own Albinostan and cleanse it of anyone who doesn't belong.'

Benjamin considered this idea. 'But that would mean anyone who wasn't as palely pigmented as I am. And that wouldn't help. Because under this white skin I'm actually a real black African.'

CHAPTER 27

Comoros Islands, 1993–94

The run of luck that had been with Jimfish and Zoran promptly deserted them soon after they set sail from Dar es Salaam. Their idea had been to cruise in easy stages down the east African coast to Cape Town, but wild storms pushed their small craft much further east. When they ran out of fuel, they drifted helplessly for many days, their water almost gone.

So it was with enormous relief, early one morning, that they spotted, rising from the water, the lush forests and sugary sands of an island.

Evidently, their boat had been spotted, perhaps even expected, because a flotilla of dugout canoes paddled out to greet them and took them in tow. When their craft was brought safely through the breakers and on to the beach, crowds of islanders were waiting and broke into applause.

A man stepped forward. He identified himself as the Mayor and read a prepared speech.

'Welcome, friends, to the Comoros, our constellation of islands. We are thrilled to have American soldiers amongst us. Even if there are just two of you for now – no doubt whole brigades will follow soon.'

The crowd broke into song and welcomed them with several verses of 'The Star-Spangled Banner'.

Zoran the Serb whispered to Jimfish: 'They have seen the Stars and Stripes painted on our boat.'

'We must correct the impression,' said Jimfish.

'I don't think it will help,' said Zoran the Serb.

But Jimfish felt duty-bound to clear up the misunderstanding.

'I am sorry to say, friends, that we are not Americans.'

'I am devastated,' said the Mayor. 'Everyone was happy to know that the legendary US marines were invading us. We've heard that they stormed ashore on the beaches of Somalia to give hope back to the Somali people and we prayed that we were next on their list, for the restoration of that precious quality. But with your help, all is not lost. The markings on your landing craft mean you must be in close touch with American fighting forces and we beg you to put in a good word for us.'

'But why would you want the Americans to invade?' Zoran asked. 'Their intervention in Somalia was a disaster. The United States lost more men in a single firefight in the streets of Mogadishu than at any time since their invasion of Vietnam. Their helicopters were shot out of the sky and the naked bodies of their soldiers were dragged through the streets by jeering mobs.'

'Look at it from our point of view,' said the Mayor. 'Over the centuries these Comoros Islands have been invaded by Arab slavers, Dutch privateers, German adventurers, Portuguese explorers and French imperialists – not to mention any number of pirates, from Davy Jones to Edward England – and I can't imagine why the Americans would be worse than any of the others. Ours are very lovely islands, where you will find dhows and dugongs, vanilla trees and volcanoes, spices and a rich array of marine life. But what we're really famous for are military coups. In the last decade or so, since independence from France, we have averaged one army rebellion every year. The ruling regime is overthrown, only for the next one to go the same way itself a short while later. And this trend shows no signs of stopping. On the map the official name for our scattering of islands may be the Comoros, but to lots of people we are simply the "Coup-Coup" Islands. How can an American invasion be any worse than all the others?

'Right now we are just recovering from our latest coup attempt. A group of morris dancers arrived on a regular commercial flight from South Africa, come to share with Comorans the delights of English country pursuits. But when a customs official asked one of the dancers to open his case, we found, not the usual flummery-mummery of morris dancers – bell pads, handkerchiefs, sticks and swords – but automatic weapons, grenade launchers and mortars. These so-called morris dancers packed more fire-power in their rucksacks than our entire defence force. We tried to arrest them, there was a firefight, they hijacked their passenger plane, still on the tarmac, and flew back to South Africa, where, no doubt, they will be welcomed as heroes. Happily for us, we captured two of the mercenary morris men and we were about to shoot them this very morning when your craft was spotted and we postponed their execution, which we will return to right now. You are very welcome to come along and watch the proceedings.'

Jimfish and Zoran had no great wish to watch an execution, but, having disappointed the Comorans once already, it seemed impolite to refuse the invitation.

The two captured mercenaries were being held in the small jail in the middle of town, and when the condemned men were led out into the yard to be shot, Jimfish could not believe his eyes, for there – thinner, older, but still with a fierce glint in his eye – was none other than his old teacher Soviet Malala, whom he knew to have been shot in faraway Ukraine. And, manacled to him, his beard now regrown to its old bushy bulk, was Deon Arlow, brother to Lunamiel and Commandant of Superior Solutions, whom Jimfish himself had shot through the heart. Two men he had known to be dead were being led before a firing squad to be killed all over again.

'Stop! Stop!' Jimfish cried, pulling out his bag of rough diamonds just as the Mayor was about to give the order to fire. 'I will pay you whatever ransom you name for these prisoners!' and he poured a heap of jewels into the outstretched palm of the Mayor, who was only too happy to accept his offer, the Comoros Islanders being amongst the poorest people in the world.

Jimfish rushed over to the prisoners, released them and hugged his old teacher Soviet Malala.

'How can this be? You died at Chernobyl. I saw it with my own eyes when you fell to the firing squad in distant Pripyat.'

'That is what happened, yes,' said Soviet Malala, 'but the soldiers in the firing squad, you'll remember, were very drunk and made several botched attempts before they even hit me. Then I was taken to the city morgue, where a local doctor found me and – never having seen a black man before in the Ukraine, and thinking, as many people in the Soviet Union did, that you should never pass up a windfall that might be saleable to someone, some day, somehow – he decided he would take me to a taxidermist, have me stuffed and put on display at travelling shows; or, otherwise, he might perhaps save my hide and sell it as shoe leather, which, like soap, toilet paper, oranges, grain and bath plugs, was in very short supply across the Soviet Union. Imagine his surprise as he was examining me to see what damage the bullets of the firing squad had done, when he found I was still breathing. He was very happy, knowing I was almost certainly worth more alive than dead, and so he tended my wounds and nursed me back to health.

'I lived with this good man when the Soviet Union was in a terrible state, after the Chernobyl disaster. The Communist Party was looking desperately for ways to salvage its reputation and, since I was a more committed believer than anyone else, I found myself a speaker at Party rallies to celebrate the Marxist cause, the Bolshevik Revolution, the triumph of the masses and the victory of the lumpenproletariat. But my efforts were doomed. The Communist Party collapsed and was officially dissolved by Gorbachev, and the Soviet Union ceased to exist.

'I found myself a solitary African in the new Russia,

where skinheads assaulted me for being black, and pusillanimous politicians were too embarrassed to even mention the names of Marx and Lenin and Stalin, the heroes of the lumpenproletariat. Luckily, I knew that one of the few places left on earth where original Communist beliefs had not altered since Stalin's time, and where the Party had taken a decision to ignore the collapse of Communism around the world, was my own country of South Africa, and I decided to go home. I won't bore you with the story of my travels across Eastern Europe, but I had got as far as Sierra Leone when I met this man here' – he pointed at the Commandant – 'who was recruiting strategic contractors for Superior Solutions.'

Jimfish, though moved by the story of his teacher's plight in Russia, was dismayed by his unseemly liaison with Deon Arlow: 'But by joining his morris-dancer coup, you collaborated in an invasion of another African state, the islands of the Comoros. And that, surely, was completely counter to your socialist faith?'

'Not at all,' said Soviet Malala. 'Are you familiar with Marx's Sixth Thesis on Feuerbach?'

Jimfish was sorry to admit he had never heard of it.

'It concludes that all individuals are elements of the social collective, and since all freedom is determined by history, this means I was predestined to join Superior Solutions and thus to invade the Comoros Islands.'

'But you were free to refuse to do so, surely?' Jimfish cried.

'In Marxist terms, freedom means facing the fact that we are historically determined,' said Soviet Malala, 'and in any event, it was of the first importance that I return to South Africa by any means possible, so as to speed the coming revolution and energize the masses.'

'And what about you?' Jimfish turned to Deon Arlow. 'When I last saw you, you were undisputably dead – and I should know, because I was the one who shot you through the heart.'

'Certainly you shot me though the heart and, in other circumstances, that would have been fatal. But remember, Superior Solutions is a proudly South African enterprise and heart transplants were pioneered by South Africans, and the procedures are well tried and tested. We had in our medical team some of the best surgeons in the world. What slows down the number of transplants is the lack of heart donors, but luckily the carnage of Sierra Leone's civil war meant there was never a problem in finding me a good young heart. Better by far than the one I lost to you.'

'Are you telling me that your transplant involved an African heart?' asked Jimfish.

'Exactly so,' said Deon Arlow. 'I leased my sister Lunamiel to the Zairean Minister of Mines to show that white South Africans are open to constructive business across the Mother Continent. And what better proof that old prejudices are over than the fact that, inside here' – he touched his chest – 'beats a true, new African heart.'

CHAPTER 28

Pretoria, South Africa, 1994

After the coup attempt by Deon Arlow's troupe of fake morris dancers, air travel from the Comoros, always intermittent, was even more irregular than usual, and Jimfish and his party were forced to wait weeks before a flight would be available to take them back to South Africa.

It was during this time that Jimfish made a discovery. Besides vanilla, spices and military coups, for most Comorians fishing was the only way to earn a scant living. Anglers paddled their dugout canoes close to the shore and used long hand-lines of plaited cotton, cunningly baited and dropped deep. It was an uncertain, risky livelihood and earned fishermen barely enough to feed their families.

However, they told him of a particular catch so valuable that to hook one was like winning the lottery. They called this fish the '*gombessa*'. It was coloured a beautiful steely blue, shading into mauve, with dabs of white, sported four little legs and lived hidden in deep sea caves. The *gombessa* grew as tall as a man of average height, weighed about the same and had wonderful powers: it could stand on its head and swim upside down or backwards, using its four little legs.

Jimfish knew instantly what this fish was. His mind went back to Port Pallid, where the old skipper had found him on the harbour wall, and to those blissful moments he had spent with Lunamiel in the orchard of Sergeant Arlow, only to be violently driven from the policeman's garden to wander the world for ten whole years, never managing to land on the right side of history. How strange to come so far, to these islands, in the Mozambique channel between Tanzania and Madagascar, only to find himself hearing of the same fish as the old trawler skipper had once caught off the Chalumna river mouth. A fossil that everyone believed dead for millions of years turned out to be alive and swimming. Here it was again, close beside him, in the waters of the Comoros, and it meant things couldn't be too bad.

'*A fish out of water, like me,*' Jimfish repeated to himself.

The islanders suggested to Jimfish that with limitless wealth in his bag of rough diamonds he could invest in a flotilla of dugouts to comb the known coelacanth fishing grounds. They were sure to strike lucky. At present just two or three coelacanths were hooked each year, the price was steadily rising and a fisherman could earn as much as three years' income with a single sale. International aquaria, trophy hunters and marine museums vied to own a coelacanth. In Asia a market was opening up for the golden fluid from its spinal cord, which was was rumoured to add years to life.

Jimfish listened politely, but declined. For a man who

had been tortured in a shipping container in Matabeleland, confined in a Soviet penal colony, locked up in East Berlin, captured by Somali kidnappers and netted and nearly sliced to pieces in an albino auction room in Tanzania the very idea of hunting down another living creature to supply demented hypochondriacs in the Asian market with the spinal fluid of a fish said to be the elixir of life, was more than he could bear.

Besides, he had other things on his mind. From Deon Arlow he had heard alarming news of Lunamiel, who he had left to fend for herself in the terrible civil war in Liberia. Deon Arlow reported that just before he had set off to topple the government of the Comoros he had seen his sister, and it was a sad tale he had to tell.

'My sister has not had an easy time. If you remember the recent wars in Liberia you will know that President Samuel Doe was done to death by Prince Johnson, who in turn was ousted in the race to be president by Charles Taylor, whose election promise – "I killed your ma. I killed your pa. Vote for me or I'll kill you too!" – was one of the most effective slogans in living memory. After these elections, Brigadier Bare-Butt suddenly declared himself celibate and gave up my sister. He renounced politics for religion, put aside his naked ways, threw away his AK-47 and dissolved his Small Boys Unit, in their fright wigs and wedding frocks, to go on the road, preaching the gospel of charity and forgiveness to the war-weary people of Liberia.

'My dear sister was reduced to begging in the streets of Monrovia, and would still be there but for an amazing stroke of luck. A visiting businessman – hearing her accent when she asked for bread – knew instantly that she was one of us. This good Samaritan turned out to be an important official in the party which will soon form the new government of South Africa. He rescued Lunamiel, flew her home and gave her a job in his Johannesburg mansion, where she works today as a cleaning maid.'

Hearing this, Jimfish had one thought in his mind: to get home and find Lunamiel – and when he heard that regular flights to South Africa had started again he was overjoyed.

The Comorians were sorry to see Jimfish and his friends leaving and a big crowd accompanied the four travellers to the airport, where the Mayor thanked each of them personally for their help and advice in showing his compatriots how things were done in the wider world. He praised Jimfish for sailing a United States warship to the Comoros Islands on a first official visit; he complimented Soviet Malala for his uplifting lectures on rage, rocket fuel and how to land on the right side of history; he commended Zoran the Serb for suggesting the Comoros Islands should splinter into a constellation of micro-states along ex-Yugoslavian lines, each with its own flag, army and dictionary; and he promised to bear in mind Deon Arlow's offer to fly in 'conflict control contractors' by helicopter gunship at the first signs of a fresh army coup.

'We plan to preserve your inflatable landing craft as a memento of your visit,' the Mayor said. 'When you next meet the American military, please tell them that if ever they plan a fresh humanitarian intervention – or a short, sharp surgical strike in some distant, deserving corner of the world – they are welcome here, whenever their busy schedule permits.'

So it was on the tenth of May 1994 – a decade after Jimfish had left for what Soviet Malala called 'the outside world' – that the flight from the Comoros, carrying Jimfish, Soviet Malala, Zoran the Serb and Deon Arlow, touched down in Johannesburg. They found the airport teeming with presidents, kings, queens, princes, pop stars and potentates, and they very soon understood the reason for the excitement. Their timing could not have been more auspicious: Nelson Mandela was about to be inaugurated as the first freely chosen President of South Africa.

The travellers joined the cavalcade and were swept along in the human tide of tens of thousands, making their way by road and rail and on foot to the swearing-in ceremony, which was to take place in Pretoria at the Union Buildings, a ponderous, red-roofed government office which reminded Zoran of similar piles in his native ex-Yugoslavia.

'It looks to me,' said Zoran, 'like a cross between a giant penitentiary and a mammoth post office.'

Soviet Malala explained to Zoran that the Union Buildings had been designed by the British at the end of the Boer War, after they had destroyed the two Boer republics of the Transvaal and the Free State, thereby securing South Africa's immense gold and diamond reserves for the city of London. It was a triumphal statement in sandstone.

Deon Arlow was pleasantly surprised to hear Soviet Malala taking this view.

'I never expected to hear you sympathizing with the suffering of Afrikaners in the Boer War,' he said.

'But it wasn't really a war – it was more of a smash-and-grab robbery,' said Soviet Malala. 'The British saw themselves as aristocrats, when, really, they were simply armed thieves, highwaymen hungry for loot. They saw the Boers as troglodytes, brute Neanderthals who never evolved into a higher order of humanity. They were a problem to be solved. Finally. So the British solved it by burning their farms, and then trucked their women and kids to concentration camps, where thousands died of disease, hunger and heartbreak.'

Deon Arlow was so moved to hear the fate of his people described with such sympathy by a black Communist that he could only nod vigorously as he fought back his tears.

'Wasn't it a crying shame, then,' Soviet Malala continued, 'once the British left and handed the country back to your lot, that Boers treated blacks in exactly the way the British had dealt with them? Now it was us who were your barbarians, troglodytes, Neanderthals, hewers of wood and drawers of water, useless appendages, monkeys, menials, miscreants or servants. Or caged pets kept for your pleasure. Or slave labour in what you liked to call a "Union" – where we did the work, while you lot prayed and picnicked in front of this triumphant erection in sandstone we see right here, always telling yourselves you were God's Chosen People.'

Anxious to calm things down on such an auspicious day, Jimfish said, 'Well, what better place to begin the new South Africa? The old order is gone. Defeated. The British robbed the Boers, and then they did in the blacks. Now that's all over. Finished. No one needs to be done in any more, right?'

'It was never a defeat!' Deon Arlow shouted. 'We got here through a negotiated settlement. It was a truce between us whites, who decided not to fight to a standstill, and you black guys, who didn't have the capacity to win. It was a compromise.'

'It was the victory of the lumpenproletariat – fighting under the banner of the glorious liberation movements – over the neo-liberal, semi-fascist, racist, white-settler entity!' cried Soviet Malala.

'Pretty damn useless liberation movements! You guys couldn't fight your way out of a paper bag! Or run a bath – never mind a revolution!' retorted Deon Arlow.

'It sounds to me very like a typical stitch-up between elites,' Zoran the Serb suggested. 'When a nasty civil war tears a neighbourhood apart, the neighbours get busy and kill each other. When it's over and the dust settles, those at the bottom of the heap find they're still there and the guys who did the deal are swigging champagne in the name of the people.'

Soviet Malala's response was lost in the jubilation as Nelson Mandela took the oath and the long-term prisoner whose name no one had been allowed to mention was transformed into a president to whom everyone pledged their love and respect.

When Mandela said, 'Let there be justice for all. Let there be peace for all. Let there be work, bread, water and salt for all,' he spoke to the heart of the country.

When he saluted his predecessor, F. W. de Klerk, once his jailer, who had made for himself a place in history, everyone cheered.

When he promised, 'Never, never and never again shall it be that our beautiful land will again experience the oppression of one by another,' strangers hugged each other.

And when he declared that neither white nor black would ever again rule over the other, but that a Rainbow Nation was to be forged from old hatreds, he summed up what the country wanted to hear more than anything in the world.

In the great amphitheatre of the Union Buildings, across its vast lawns, in the streets, suburbs and townships of the capital, and across the country, citizens danced, prayed and sang.

At last Jimfish felt he had arrived at that moment on the right side of history. But what had brought him to this point? Not the high-octane rage that is the rocket fuel of the lumpenproletariat. There was no anger in Mandela and no recrimination.

Jimfish would have liked to ask Soviet Malala for his frank opinion of just what all this meant. But his old teacher was watching Fidel Castro with intense concentration, as if hoping he would say something to inject a little revolutionary fire into the hazy delirium of rainbows and reconciliation. But El Commandante, who sat on the podium, among queens, princes, presidents, civil rights leaders, prelates, pop stars and a brace of bemedalled dictators, kept his counsel, and so did Soviet Malala.

CHAPTER 29

Jimfish had just one goal now: to be reunited with Lunamiel. Helped by Soviet Malala's connections in the new government, being a devout member of the Communist Party, Jimfish soon knew the name of the good Samaritan who had rescued Lunamiel in Monrovia and brought her back to South Africa. Now a minister in the presidency, he lived in a grand house in the tree-lined northern suburbs of Johannesburg, behind tall walls topped with razor wire and electrified fencing, patrolled around the clock by armed guards.

Having announced their presence on the intercom, Jimfish and his friends waited while the CCTV cameras checked them over. The automatic steel gates opened, the dogs were kennelled, they were signed in by the gatekeeper in his wooden sentry box, passed through the metal detectors, and a bodyguard escorted them into the minister's study.

'It is very like visiting a prisoner,' said Zoran.

'Better,' said Deon. 'State-of-the-art electric fencing,

lovely-looking razor wire, serious firearms on the guards and infrared beams. I'll bet they've got sound sensors buried under the walls to keep out tunnellers.'

'But it's all perfectly normal around here,' said the minister, clearly embarassed. 'As a member of the new government I had to move into a neighbourhood that was once the sole preserve of our former masters. To show the flag. But I felt a lot safer when I lived in a black township.'

Jimfish sympathized. The man had been parachuted into the world of the rich white classes – at once so pleasurable and so like a prison.

'We are here to see your maid, Lunamiel,' said Jimfish, 'the girl you rescued in Monrovia.'

The minister was more embarrassed than ever. 'I'm afraid that's impossible. She's left.'

'But why?' Jimfish was horrified.

'I don't know why,' said the minister. 'We treated her kindly, paid her promptly, fed and clothed her, gave her an afternoon off once a week. But then, you know how it is with domestic staff, one minute they're fine – the next they've gone. Maybe she had challenges' – the minister paused delicately – 'coming from a formerly privileged group.'

Jimfish was flummoxed. 'I don't know how you can call her privileged.'

'He means white,' said Soviet Malala briskly.

'I must find her,' said Jimfish. 'Please help me.'

The minister sighed. 'I hear she's living in a shanty town. In a shack of tin and tarpaulin. Without lights or running water and just a bucket toilet. I'll give you the address. If you see her, please say that her job is still open. She's a good girl and I was sorry to lose her.'

The informal settlement where they would find Lunamiel, the minister warned them, was crowded with poor whites and notorious for drugs, robbery, rape and drug addiction. Tour buses took black families to see for themselves what happened to whites who had lost everything; much as whites once toured black townships for glimpses of life on the other side of the colour bar.

The minister had not overstated the conditions in the camp where Jimfish and his companions found Lunamiel stooped over a zinc washing tub. It was not easy to recognize her. She looked so much older and her luscious skin, once as downy as a ripe peach, was deeply lined and she had lost much weight.

'My darling Lunamiel! How do you manage to live here?'

Jimfish put his arms around her and she felt as thin as a starving bird.

'As you see, I take in laundry,' she told him.

Soviet Malala was not particularly sympathetic. 'She comes from a life of pampered privilege. Too bad if she learns how our people had to live.'

Zoran the Serb said simply, 'Isn't it strange how things go around?'

Jimfish was so overcome with guilt that he covered his long-lost love in kisses and did not notice the looks he was getting from her brother Deon.

'My poor, dear Lunamiel! Can you ever forgive me for

abandoning you to the mercies of Brigadier Bare-Butt?'

'It's an ill wind that blows no good,' said Lunamiel sweetly. 'It was when he was with me that the brigadier heard the call of the Lord and turned overnight from homicidal maniac into a holy man.'

'God works in mysterious ways,' said Jimfish.

'Amen to that. And nowhere are His ways more of a mystery than right here,' said Lunamiel. 'The brigadier passed me on, briefly, to a Rwandan politician of the Hutu tribe, but the poor man was far too busy with the civil war in his country and soon dropped me. I was on the streets when this rich South African saved me, flew me home and gave me a job amongst his domestic staff.'

'What generosity!' cried Jimfish. 'And he wants you back. Your job is still open!'

Lunamiel shuddered. 'Never! I don't deny he was a kind employer. I had my own room in the backyard, a spoon, an enamel plate and a tin mug. But I had to scrub, wash, iron, cook, sew and look after my employer's children six days a week – things no normal white woman has ever in her life done for herself, never mind doing it for people who just the other day were doing it for me, whose mother kept a fleet of staff and assigned separate servants to each hand when her nails needed painting. Worse still, my boss had advanced political views and his domestic employees reflected the demographics of our country. He kept ten black staff to one of me and the others mocked me for being useless at the simplest jobs, telling me I hadn't a clue how to do anything except give orders. They kept asking how it was that whites had run South Africa for so long when we were so useless. One night I ran away and here I am in this shanty town for very poor whites, whose numbers grow each day, but at least I'm back amongst my own people.'

Listening to the story of Lunamiel's decline and fall, Zoran sighed his Serbian sigh. 'This talk of togetherness is all very well,' he said. 'But it's going to take a long time before it works.'

Soviet Malala regarded Lunamiel's plight as nothing less than the punishment the settler entity deserved. 'You've at last felt the angry lash of the masses,' he said. 'The rage of lumpenproletariat has blown you on to the rubbish dump of history.'

'I don't care about any of that,' said Jimfish, and he took Lunamiel in his arms. 'I have deserted you too often, and I will marry you tomorrow and we'll go home to Port Pallid!'

That was when Deon Arlow stepped forward and angrily separated the lovers.

'Now, listen here,' he said. 'I'm ready to adapt and I'll never oppress another because of race or colour. As our new President said in his speech, what is past is past. OK? I love every last colour in the rainbow, I swear to God. But I also swore on the family Bible that I would never let my sister marry a black man, not even one who might be white. Over my dead body.'

Lunamiel flung herself at her brother's feet and begged him to reconsider.

Deon Arlow repeated that Lunamiel descended from the purest Dutch and German and Scandinavian stock;

she was Aryan to the nth degree, and love across the colour bar was a rainbow too far.

Jimfish wheeled on him, yanking his pistol from its python-skin holster.

'Aryan?' he said. 'What nonsense! Your family probably descended from slaves and pirates, and Hottentots, Malays and Bushmen. If there is any German or Dutch blood in you it's from the press-ganged scum of the Berlin gutters and the dross of the Amsterdam pot-houses. Rogues who sailed to the Cape of Good Hope, slept with their slaves and told themselves they were the master race. You leased my dearest Lunamiel to a brace of black Congolese cabinet ministers and a naked Liberian brigadier, without thinking twice. Well, I saved your life in the Comoros and brought you home. I've already shot you dead once and I'll happily do it again!'

But Soviet Malala stepped between them just in time and took Jimfish aside.

'I have a better use for him,' he said. 'Yes, he's an unreconstructed racist of the old school: cynical, meretricious and stupid. But the old white mindset aside, since his recent transplant he has an African heart. In the new South Africa we need people able to speak out of both sides of their mouths. His combination of boneheadedness and *ubuntu* would make him an excellent ambassador.'

And so it was – after Soviet Malala dropped a few words in the ears of his powerful friends in the governing party – that Deon Arlow was appointed ambassador to Rwanda, where terrible massacres had begun. There it was that the founder of Superior Solutions would come face to face with the wholesale murder of the minority Tutsis by the majority Hutus, and witness the racial cataclysm that those of his kind had been ready to risk – and promote – in South Africa, where, for decades, one tribe ruthlessly ground all others into the dust and where bloodshed of Rwandan proportions was about to happen, had not the miracle of messy compromise arrived at the last moment.

Everyone praised the brilliant idea of sending Deon Arlow to Rwanda – except Zoran, who thought it might make matters worse.

'At the moment in that sad place Tutsis are being slaughtered by Hutus,' he said. 'But what if the tide turns and the Hutus are stopped and defeated? Won't Tutsis take their turn at the top table and make life hell for the Hutus? They will need arms, advice and military contractors. That's when Ambassador Arlow's former skills as Commandant of Superior Solutions will come in handy.'

Soviet Malala announced that he was shocked by such cynicism.

'Why call me cynical when I am just being Serbian?' Zoran wanted to know.

'Because there are things people don't want to hear,' said Jimfish.

'Or to say,' said Zoran the Serb. 'And when that happens you know the new regime has started shutting down debate.'

Soviet Malala, who was rising fast in the ruling party, was deployed to warn Zoran that while positive criticism was welcome and essential and the democratic right of every citizen, if he insisted on sowing discord the Serb should not complain if some patriot gave him (and here Soviet Malala used a local word that covered everything from a slap on the wrist to a bullet in the heart) a good '*klap*' and bundled him back to Belgrade. There was no room for a sceptical Serb – or anyone else who failed to applaud the miracle of peace and harmony that was the Rainbow Nation. Negative thinking must be monitored, just as the press, which had been showing signs of irresponsible behaviour, would be made to put its house in order. The beloved country was a miracle in the making and that was official.

Zoran was amused in his gloomy way. 'Just one miracle in the making? Why so shy? I can give you a few more. Here's Miracle Number Two: nowhere can you meet any white person who will admit to backing the old system of locking people in the prison of their skin. People who stewed in murderous racial hatred now lose themselves in a haze of sentimental self-congratulation and officially endorsed national amnesia. Next comes Miracle Number Three: a ruling party with a massive majority, claiming the right to rule until the day of judgement, turns overnight into a fractious bunch of finger-wagging scolds, frightened of their own shadow, terrified of dissent, seeing enemies everywhere and threatening to shut them up.'

'Foreigners are always frightened at the way we do things in this country,' said Soviet Malala.

'I'm not a foreigner, I'm a Serb,' said Zoran. 'And what I'm feeling is not fear, it's déjà vu.'

Soon, when Soviet Malala began leading marches of youthful supporters chanting their promise to kill for the Party, Zoran decided it was time to pack for Belgrade.

'So God works in mysterious ways in many places,' he said. 'But He is at the very top of His game in the new South Africa.'

'I'm really sorry to see you go back to the violence, corruption and hatred of war-torn ex-Yugoslavia,' said Jimfish, hugging his gloomy friend.

'Don't give it a thought,' said Zoran the Serb. 'When I see where you guys are heading, I think maybe we're not doing so badly, after all.'

CHAPTER 30

Port Pallid, South Africa, 1994

Jimfish and Lunamiel married and returned to peaceful Port Pallid on the Indian Ocean, where, in the mad mid-1980s the trawler skipper had one day found a boy on the harbour wall. They bought the old man's house and took over his boat, the *Lady Godiva*.

Port Pallid had remained what it had always been, a rocky knoll jutting into the Indian Ocean, a thumb poked into a cerulean eye, where no one now was to be found who had ever in their lives believed in the old religion of race and colour; and no one remembered their pledge to the former leader, Piet the Weapon, 'to die for you till kingdom come'. But everyone believed instead in the saintliness of the man who had spent all those years on Robben Island.

Jimfish often sailed to the fishing grounds of the Chalumna river mouth, where the old skipper had seen his first coelacanth, and, as the boat rocked on the water, he knew that deep down in the ocean there lived a beautiful blue fish with four legs that could stand on its head and swim backwards.

'A very queer fish indeed. Just like me.'

The thought gave him comfort and pleasure. The coelacanth had kept going when everyone had taken it for dead. But Jimfish knew now that it was being hunted and desired, and if this went on, the creature that had been alive milions of years before humans were even thought of, would disappear again, and this time there would be no miracle return.

Jimfish would ask Lunamiel: 'If the coelacanth knew this, what would it think?'

Lunamiel said maybe it would think that it had not been a good idea, many millions of years ago, for an early relative to have struggled ashore on its four legs and stayed.

'Because here we are,' said Lunamiel, 'and that is not good news for the coelacanth.'

In the deep calm of the little fishing port there seemed room for everyone, and Jimfish and Lunamiel were very happy.

It was quite an event, then, to see a column of Mercedes slide into town one day, each as long and as big and as shiny as the one in which Jimfish and Lunamiel had fled Zaire. A platoon of young men jumped from the cars and began marching down the main road of the town, led by none other than Soviet Malala. In place of the Lenin cap he had once worn long ago, he now sported a cherry-red beret and T-shirt emblazoned with the letters FFF. As they marched, they sang to a tune Jimfish thought he remembered:

Soviet Malala, he's the one!
We'll fight for him till kingdom come!
And die for him, in due course!
Viva the Fiscal Fighting Force!

'What's left to fight for?' Jimfish asked his old teacher. 'I thought you had won?'

Soviet Malala adjusted his red beret. 'Nothing has changed for the masses. This so-called new regime is just the old regime in disguise. My Fiscal Fighting Force will destroy these sell-outs and traitors, these black masks on white faces.'

Jimfish was as confused as ever he had been in the days when he sat at Soviet Malala's feet in the garden of Sergeant Arlow, absorbing his philosophy of prolo-fisc-freedo-mism. He appeared to have everything he wanted and yet he seemed angrier than ever – but now it was with those he had sworn to fight and die for.

'Down with the Party!' Soviet Malala punched the air.

'Have you left your own movement?' Jimfish asked.

'It has left me,' said Soviet Malala. 'When I remind them that rage is the rocket fuel of the lumpenproletariat, what do they do? They tell me I need anger-management classes. Come and join us, Jimfish! Nothing is more important than saving the lumpenproletariat!'

'That may be so,' said Jimfish, 'but I'd be happy if I could save the coelacanth.'

NOTE ON THE AUTHOR

Christopher Hope was born in Johannesburg in 1944. He is the author of nine novels and one collection of short stories, including *Kruger's Alp*, which won the Whitbread Prize for Fiction, *Serenity House*, which was shortlisted for the 1992 Booker Prize, *My Mother's Lovers* and *Shooting Angels*, published by Atlantic Books in 2012 to great acclaim. He is also a poet and playwright, and the author of the celebrated memoir *White Boy Running* (1988).